Ablaze

Dallas Fire & Rescue

Paige Tyler

Cover Design by Kim Killion Designs
Editing by Wizards in Publishing

ISBN-13: 978-1543299465

ISBN-10: 1543299466

Dedication

With special thanks to my extremely patient and understanding husband, without whose help and support I couldn't have pursued my dream job of becoming a writer. You're my sounding board, my idea man, my critique partner, and the absolute best research assistant any girl could ask for!
Thank you.

The heat is on...

Paramedic Lexi Fletcher is thrilled to transfer to Station 58. For one thing, her commute time is half of what it used to be. For another, Station 58 has a much better facility and far more exciting calls. It doesn't hurt that Dane Chandler, the firefighter she's been crushing on since joining Dallas and Rescue, works there. Okay, to tell the truth, maybe Dane is the biggest reason she requested the move!

But just when things with Dane start to heat up, Lexi's dream job takes a turn in the freaky direction. Patients she's been bringing to the hospital are turning up dead, even though they were in stable condition when she dropped them off. Her instincts are screaming there's something fishy going on, but she can't figure out what it is, and she can't get anyone to believe her—except Dane.

Can he help her find the killer and stop him from striking again, or will Lexi become the target of a madman?

Chapter One

LEXI FLETCHER CURSED under her breath as she and fellow paramedic Trent Barnes rushed over to the burning apartment complex to take the older man off firefighter Jax Malloy's hands. Crap, it felt like the flames were searing her skin—and they were a dozen feet away. Giving them a quick nod, Jax turned and ran back into the raging inferno engulfing the building like it wasn't there at all. Then again, that's what firefighters did. They ran into burning buildings when everyone else ran out.

The old man was coughing so hard Lexi thought he might pass out before they got him to their rescue vehicle. She and Trent draped his arms around their shoulders and hauled butt over to the ambulance. The moment they had the man on a gurney, Lexi reached for the oxygen mask while Trent checked his vitals.

"Contusion to the top of the head," she said to Trent as she fitted the mask over the older man's face. "Possible concussion."

After Trent took the man's pulse, the dark-haired paramedic moved up and began checking the man's eyes, ears, and nose with a small flashlight. "Sir, I'm going to ask you a few questions. You don't have to say anything out loud, just nod your head. Do you understand?"

The man kept the oxygen mask pressed to his face as he nodded. He was still coughing a little, but not nearly as badly as before.

As Trent went into the concussion protocol, asking about blurred vision and ringing in the ears, Lexi checked the man for other injuries. She kept one eye on the burning apartment building while she worked, praying there weren't more people in there. The fire was bad enough for dispatch to call in two full stations worth of firefighters, pumper engines, ladder trucks, and rescue vehicles. That wasn't counting the three other reserve rescue vehicles there to take care of the injured if needed.

While there were a lot of people who required medical attention, it wasn't nearly as bad as it could have been. Thankfully, a teenaged boy had smelled smoke and pulled the alarm then gone around banging on doors and shouting for everyone to get out before the fire had gotten too out of control. She had no idea who the kid was, but he deserved a medal.

There were still a lot of firefighters in there though, some going apartment to apartment checking for anyone who hadn't been able to get out while others tried to vent the fire away from the structure. With a fire this size, both operations were extremely dangerous. Lexi tried to mentally keep a running count of how many firefighters had gone inside and how many had come out.

She worried about all of them, but she had to admit she paid special attention to the firefighters from Station 58. Those were her people. They worked together, lived together, laughed and cried together—they were her family. Until they were all out of there safe and sound, she was going to worry about them.

Lexi and Trent were lining the gurney up so they could slide the mobile bed and the old man on it into the back of their rescue vehicle when she caught a flash of movement out of the corner of her eye. She turned to see two big firefighters coming out of the smoke and flames enveloping the front of the building, dragging an equally tall firefighter between them. Her breath caught. While it should have been impossible to identify anyone in the turnout gear the DF&R issued to every firefighter in the city, she instinctively knew those three were from Station 58. Worse, she feared she knew exactly who the tall guy in the middle was.

Since she and Trent had their patient

ready to roll to the hospital, another paramedic team should have stepped up to tend to the injured firefighter, but every single rescue team had their hands full at the moment. Trent must have realized that, too, because he shooed her in the direction of the three men from Station 58.

"Go take care of him," Trent said. "He's one of ours, and Wayne isn't in crisis."

It took Lexi a moment to figure out that Wayne was the older man. When had Trent learned his name?

Nodding, she grabbed her emergency bag and ran toward the firefighters, waving her arm to get their attention. She reached them as Jax and fellow firefighter Tory Wilcox helped Dane Chandler to the ground and got his air bottle pack off his back.

Lexi dropped to her knees beside the big firefighter and quickly unfastened his helmet and slipped his SCBA mask off. She didn't hear much in the way of escaping oxygen, meaning Dane had already been close to running out of air even before Jax and Tory brought him out. That scared the hell out of her. A firefighter was trained to leave a fire well before his tank approached empty. The only reason he would stay longer was to save a life, or if he was in trouble.

She skimmed Dane's Nomex fire hood off next, once again struck by how incredibly handsome he was. Dark haired, with brown eyes the color of espresso, he had a strong jaw and the most kissable lips she'd ever seen. Lexi gave herself a mental shake, forcing herself to stop thinking about Dane as a man and instead focus on him as a patient and check for injuries. He seemed a little dazed, but she couldn't see anything obvious.

"What happened to him?" she asked, glancing at Jax and Tory as they took off their masks.

"We were venting windows on the third floor," Jax said, concern clear on his face as he started undoing the jacket of Dane's turnout gear. "One second, he was standing right beside me, and the next the floor gave out under him and he fell all the way down to the second level—which was fully engulfed in fire at the time."

Lexi's eyes went wide. *Crap*.

Dane waved a hand and shook his head. Or tried to anyway. Lexi cupped his face in both hands and held him still. "You could have a concussion."

"I'm fine," Dane insisted with a frown. "I landed on the remnants of king-size bed. I even bounced when I hit."

"Right," Tory said sarcastically. "The part he's leaving out is the fact that he landed on his head on the bed's metal frame then had to smash his way through a flaming bedroom door on his way out."

This kept getting better. Or rather, worse.

Dane shrugged. "It wasn't a big deal. I have a hard head. Besides, there wasn't much left of the door to smash. Get me another bottle, and I'm ready to go back to work."

Both Jax and Tory snorted at that.

Lexi slipped her hands inside the top of Dane's turnout gear and gently pressed her fingers against his ribs and stomach looking for tender spots. While she was somewhat distracted by all the muscles she felt there, she couldn't miss the way he flinched as she glided her hands over his lower ribs. He did it again when she pressed her fingers into the muscles of his neck.

Jax saw the reaction, too, and didn't have a problem calling his friend on it. "You're not going anywhere."

"Except to the hospital in the back of my rescue vehicle," Lexi added.

She slid her hands down to check out Dane's chest and abs once more. It probably wasn't necessary since she'd already figured out he wasn't seriously injured, only heavily bruised. But she was a trained professional. That was her job.

She glanced up to see Dane regarding her with a knowing look on his face and a twinkle in his eyes. Crap, he hadn't noticed how incredibly thorough that exam had been, had he?

Dane leaned in a little closer and chuckled softly in her ear. "You know there are easier ways to get me strapped down to a bed, right?"

She felt her face heat as she realized she'd definitely been caught. But instead of feeling embarrassed, she kind of felt...challenged. It was like Dane was playing with her, waiting to see how she'd react to his over-the-top line.

Lexi was still trying to come up with a snappy comeback, which she had to admit wasn't her strong suit, when Captain Earl Stewart—their boss at Station 58—walked over to them. Nearing sixty and whipcord lean, he looked like he could still fight fires alongside the men and women under his command.

"I heard what happened," the captain said. "How bad is it?"

He was looking at Lexi as he asked the question, but it was Dane who answered. "I'm good. Ready to get back in there."

Stewart glanced at him, a scowl on his weathered face. "Was I talking to you?"

Dane opened his mouth to complain, but the captain had already turned back to Lexi. "Is he good?"

Lexi didn't even have to think about it. She wasn't going to let Dane go back in that building, no matter how much he wanted to.

"No, he's not good," she said, shaking her head. "It's nothing serious, but he needs to go to a hospital and get checked out for possible cracked ribs and neck damage."

"Captain—" Dane began, but Captain Stewart interrupted him.

"Put him in the next rescue vehicle heading to the hospital," he said to Lexi, then jabbed a finger at Dane. "That's an order."

That ended the argument. Jax told Dane that he'd come pick him up later if he needed a ride, and less than a minute later, Lexi had him in the back of the rescue vehicle with her and Wayne while Trent drove. She would have preferred Dane on a gurney, but that would have meant waiting for another vehicle and she wasn't willing to do that. So, instead, he sat beside her, listening as the older man told them about a piece of the ceiling falling down and hitting him on the head. She sat there and monitored both men's vitals as they talked about what Wayne was going to do now.

"I don't really know." The older man's face clouded. "Everything I owned was in that apartment. I don't even have any fresh clothes to put on."

"I think I can help with that," Dane said. "We have plenty of clothes people donate to our firehouse for situations like this. I'll make sure you get something to wear. Is there anyone you want me to call? Family, maybe...or friends?"

Wayne shook his head, his blue eyes sad. "Not really. Family's all gone. Friends, too. Only me, now. I don't even have any pictures of anybody anymore. They were all in my apartment."

Dane gave him a small smile. "Don't be too sure of that. Not all of the apartments are completely destroyed. There's a good chance we'll be able to get some of your stuff out of there."

Lexi wasn't too sure of that, but it was nice of Dane to give the older man some hope. It sounded like he really needed some of that right then.

As they drove to the hospital, she filled the intake forms out on the station-issued iPad, and listened in as Wayne told them about his family, friends, and a long life of travel and adventure as a sports reporter. Dane smiled at her once or twice, but mostly he sat there and listened to Wayne talk, occasionally asking questions the older man obviously wanted to answer. Wayne clearly enjoyed talking to Dane. Lexi could understand why. The big firefighter was the kind of person others were immediately drawn to. Lexi should know. She'd moved her butt all the way across town for a chance to work in the same station as Dane.

She'd had a thing for Dane from the moment she'd seen him at one of her first multi-alarm fires. Even dressed like every other firefighter there, he'd stood out. There was simply something special about him. Something more than the good looks, great body, and quick, boyish smile. After running into him at dozens of incident scenes and citywide department functions, she'd wanted to get to know him better. The problem had been getting him to notice her. She'd flirted when she'd gotten the chance, but he was a guy—which meant clueless. It didn't help that her uniform wasn't exactly the most alluring outfit she'd ever worn, and the department kind of frowned on wearing dresses and high heels during duty hours. So after talking to some of the female firefighters and paramedics at his station to make sure he wasn't involved with anyone seriously, she'd asked for a transfer to 58.

Dane hadn't been the only reason she'd requested the move, though. She wasn't that insane. Moving to Station 58 was also a good career move.

Lexi had spent the past two years working at Station 44 over on Frank Street. It was a good station with great people, but it was one of the smaller stations in the DF&R, servicing mostly single-story residential homes. The work had been okay, but she'd become a paramedic so she could help people and use the skills she'd been taught. The best way to do that was to work at a station that went on a lot of calls, and Station 58 was one of the busiest squads in the city. Their area of responsibility covered everything from small homes to fifteen-story condos, and everything in between.

Then there were the facilities. Station 58 was one of the newer houses in the city, and the company had put a lot of work and effort into making the place amazing. They had state-of-the-art showers, an awesome dayroom with a big screen TV, a killer kitchen, and comfortable beds. It also didn't hurt that Station 58 was much closer to her apartment.

So, she had a lot of good reasons for

transferring to 58. But while she'd been here over two months, and had even managed to get on the same shift as Dane, she still hadn't gotten him to notice her. In fact, checking him out after he'd fallen through the floor of a burning building was the closest she'd come to having a real moment with the man in two months.

Wow, that was sad.

Sighing, Lexi glanced out the front of the rescue vehicle to see that they'd arrived at the hospital. Trent pulled up to the sliding glass doors of the emergency center then came around to the back of the vehicle to help her with the gurney. Two nurses immediately met them inside. Trent explained the older man's condition to one nurse while Lexi filled the other in on what had happened to Dane. A few minutes later, nurses whisked both patients to exam rooms, and she and Trent were left standing in the now empty hallway.

Well, crap. She'd missed her chance to talk to Dane again. Maybe she could convince Trent to hang around for a while so they could give Dane a ride back to the station. If they got a call, dispatch could still reach them on the radio.

"Hey, what's up?"

Lexi turned to see her roommate and best friend, Melinda Turner, coming toward them. Petite, with blond hair and hazel eyes, Melinda was an emergency room nurse at the hospital.

"I'm going to check on the guy we brought in," Trent said.

Flashing Melinda a grin, he headed for the exam rooms. Melinda smiled back, openly checking out his butt as he disappeared down the hallway.

"Stop that," Lexi ordered. "He's my partner."

Melinda lifted a brow. "You planning to make a move on him?"

"No!" Lexi couldn't stop the horrified look that crossed her face. "That would be too weird. Besides, I told you, I'm interested in Dane."

Melinda shrugged. "Then there's no harm in my checking out the goods, is there?" When Lexi frowned, her friend laughed. "Don't worry. I won't put you in the position of seeing your coworker naked if he sleeps over at our place and gets up to use the bathroom in the middle of the night. I'll make sure he puts on some clothes."

Lexi shook her head. "Thanks for that image. I'll probably never get it out of my head."

"Not sure why you'd want to get a visual like that out of your head," Melinda said. "He's a hunk."

Lexi fell into step beside her friend as Melinda led the way to the frenetic madhouse that was so much a part of everyday life in this part of the hospital. Off to the side, a handsome reporter was interviewing a gray-haired doctor for a local news station.

"What's that about?" Lexi asked her friend.

Melinda glanced over at the men. "A little kid saved his family in a fire earlier tonight. He smelled smoke, woke up, and got everyone out before the place burnt to the ground. He's a hero."

There seemed to be quite a bit of that going on lately, Lexi thought, remembering the teen who'd pulled the alarm at the apartment fire Station 58 had responded to that evening.

"I've gotta get back to work," Melinda said. "See you at home after your shift?"

Lexi nodded and waved, but her friend had already gotten swallowed up in the rush of people coming and going in the emergency room. Lexi stepped aside to make way for a nurse leading a man with an arm injury past, then she slipped into the area where the exam rooms were. Although, "rooms" was probably a misnomer. They were more like alcoves partitioned off from sight by nothing more than thin, opaque curtains. She'd check in on Wayne...and hopefully Dane.

Trent was talking to Wayne's doctor when she finally figured out which alcove the older man was in. The doctor was as worried about a concussion as she'd been and decided to keep Wayne overnight. Other than that, he was fine. When Lexi mentioned Wayne's apartment was almost certainly destroyed, the doctor told them he'd come up with a reason to keep the older man an extra night or two until he had somewhere to go. It wasn't much, but it was something. At least Wayne was alive. That was the important thing.

"I'm going to check on Dane," she told Trent. "See if he's going to ride back with us."

Finding Dane took a little while, but with the help of a nurse, she located him in an alcove at the end of the hall. She cautiously peeked around the curtain to see him pulling on his DF&R-issued T-shirt. She tried not to drool as she took in the muscular pecs and rippling abs.

He caught sight of her as he was tucking in his shirt, and flashed her a grin. "Doc said I'll be fine. A couple eight hundred milligram Motrin and I'll be good as new. Like I said."

She smiled as she slipped around the curtain. While the alcoves were tiny to begin with, Dane's presence made the area seem even smaller. Not that she was complaining. Especially since it meant they had to stand close together.

"I'm glad," she said. "But that doesn't mean I wasn't right about insisting you get checked out by a doctor."

"I agree. You were doing your job. I'm good with that," he said. "Truth is, every firefighter needs an unbiased third party to step in and take decisions like that out of our hands because we're rarely going to leave the scene of a fire, not in those situations."

Lexi couldn't argue with that. She loved

the firefighters she worked with, but they could be a stubborn lot, male and female alike.

"Since we're being truthful here," he continued, "I want to say that I'm sorry if I embarrassed or offended you with that comment back at the apartment fire."

She frowned. "What comment?"

He gave her a sheepish look "You know—that stupid line about strapping me down to a bed. It sounded a lot better in my head than it did coming out of my mouth."

She waved a hand. "Don't worry about it. I know you were just messing with me."

"Actually, I was trying to be charming." He smiled, and her heart beat faster. "I've been trying to figure out how to catch your eye since you got to the five-eight, and when you started patting me down for injuries, I got a little stupid and said the first thing that popped into my head. Which, I admit, is never a good idea."

She blinked. He'd been trying to catch *her* eye?

"You know," she said. "You could have simply asked me out for coffee."

He chuckled. "Yeah, that probably would have been smarter. But I was hoping to get an idea whether there was any mutual interest on your part before I officially asked you out. I didn't want to be *that guy*, you know? The one who pesters a coworker for a date and puts her in the bad position of having to worry about how her answer will affect her job."

Lexi gaped. No wonder she hadn't been able to get his attention. He'd been too busy being worried about coming on too strong with a coworker. Could this guy get any better?

"Well, if it helps, the interest is mutual," she said softly.

He flashed her that megawatt smile again. "In that case, what do you think about grabbing that cup of coffee sometime?"

"I don't drink coffee," she said, unable to help messing with him.

Dane didn't bat an eye. "Huh. Not a big fan of it, myself. How about dinner instead?"

She grinned. "Dinner I do."

His smile broadened. "How about I pick you up tomorrow night at your place around seven?"

"Perfect," she said.

"It's a date, then."

Dane grabbed his heavy turnout coat from the back of a nearby chair. Lexi had to resist the urge to ask if he needed help getting dressed. With his wit, she didn't want to even hazard a guess how he might respond to that question.

He pushed the curtain aside then stepped back so she could go ahead of him. He glanced at her as they headed for the exit of the triage area. "Think I can get a lift back to the station? If I wait for Jax to finish up at the fire, I could be waiting for hours."

"Sure," she said. "As long as you don't

mind riding in the back on the gurney. No room up front."

He shrugged. "Fine with me, though this thing with you wanting to strap me down to a bed is starting to get me curious. Is this going to be a permanent thing with you?"

Lexi laughed. "How about we get through dinner first before we talk about straps and beds, okay?"

"Good idea—dinner first, then bed." His mouth twitched. "We probably need to wait at least an hour between eating and using any kind of restraints, though."

"I think that's swimming," she pointed out.

He made a show of considering that as the double doors slid open. "Swimming, bondage—I've heard it both ways."

Lexi was wondering if Dane knew he'd quoted a line from her favorite TV show when Trent, who was leaning against the back of the rescue vehicle waiting for them, interrupted her musings.

"You riding back with us?" At Dane's nod, he jerked his thumb at the truck. "Get on the gurney and let's go."

Lexi knew it was coming before Dane even said the words. "Now I get it. This thing with the straps isn't only you. It's all paramedics."

Trent gave them a confused look. "What?"

Lexi shoved her partner toward the front of the truck. "Don't get him started."

Chapter Two

DANE STOPPED THE moment he stepped into the building and took a deep breath. Damn, it smelled good in here! It wasn't simply the cakes, cupcakes, cookies, and pies covering nearly every flat surface in the shop that had his mouth watering. It was also the aroma of the barbecue spices coming from the kitchen in the back. Skye must be making ribs or chicken...or maybe pulled pork. Either way, it made him hungry as hell.

As he crossed the front room of the building that housed his sister's catering business, he craned his neck to peek into the kitchen. It seemed even bigger than the last time he'd been here a few weeks ago. It was difficult to believe this place used to be a barn. He wouldn't be surprised if they needed to put an addition on it soon. Skye's business was growing crazy fast. When the wedding and event planners, convention centers, and corporate deliveries had started overwhelming her with requests for desserts, his sister had hired another baker and a full-time delivery driver. That had helped for a while, but then her clients had asked if she could also cater hors d'ouevres and meals too. So Skye had hired a chef and another driver as well as purchased another delivery truck, expanding her business even further.

And Dane had thought this would never work. Boy, did he feel stupid.

Five months ago, when his sister had bailed on her Wall Street job and moved back here to Dallas to open a cupcake bakery, Dane had been sure she'd lost her mind. Actually, he'd been sort of an asshole about it. But he couldn't understand why someone would turn their back on New York, a cushy job, and all that easy money to bake cupcakes of all things.

As if that wasn't enough, she'd also gotten involved then moved in with his best friend, Jax. He hadn't reacted very well to that either. Okay, in reality, he'd sort of been a complete jerk about the whole thing. But, fortunately, that stupidity had been short-lived and was all behind them now. As his sister's wedding approached, he and Skye were closer than they'd ever been in their lives, and he and Jax were closer, too. Even so, he still felt like an idiot when he remembered all the dumbass things he'd said to Jax and his sister all those months ago. That was one of the reasons he was trying to help out as much as he could with their wedding. He wanted to make up for being such a total dickweed.

In fact, that was why he was here. Skye had called and asked him to come over to give them advice about something for the wedding. Dane had no clue what he could provide insight on. When it came to weddings, he was clueless.

Jax and Skye were at the granite-topped island in the center of the shop, sampling cake. Dane might not know much about weddings, but if it involved eating cake, he was in.

"What's up?" he said. "You make too many cakes and need help eating them?"

Skye laughed, her blue eyes twinkling as she came over to hug him. "Kind of. We need your help picking out a cake for the wedding. Our taste buds are completely shot from tasting so many different ones, and we need an outside opinion."

Dane frowned. "Wait a minute. I thought you already had the cake picked out. You do realize you're getting married in a little over a week, right?"

"Skye decided she wasn't feeling the chocolate cake with raspberry mousse filling and chocolate frosting she picked out," Jax informed him, filling his fork with white cake that had fruit on the inside and peach-colored frosting. "She thinks the cake we have at our wedding needs to be the very best in the world since it will say so much about her business. We've spent the morning eating more cake than I even want to think about."

Dane wasn't sure that was possible. Grabbing a fork, he chowed down on one awesome flavor after the other, listening to his sister and best friend talk about their honeymoon plans—glamping on the shores of the Blackfoot River in Montana.

Dane paused, a forkful of red velvet cake with cream cheese frosting halfway to his mouth. "I thought you were going on a cruise."

Skye tucked her long dark hair behind her ear. "We thought about it, but Jax wanted to go camping. I told him if we were going to be sleeping in a tent on our honeymoon, it had to come with electricity, running water, and maid service. I thought that would be the end of the camping idea, but Jax found the perfect place that met both our needs. It specializes in glamorous camping—glamping. It has hiking, fishing, and horses for him, and luxurious tents with all the amenities for me, including gourmet dining, maid service twice a day, and private honeymoon tents."

Jax leaned over to kiss her. "I told you I'd find you a place you'd like."

"That's why I love you." She grinned. "Well, one of the reasons, anyway."

Dane went back to eating his cake, shaking his head at the idea of putting camping and luxurious together in the same sentence. Clearly, Skye and Jax were looking forward to it, though. A few months ago, seeing his best friend kissing his sister would have led to a fight—now he couldn't help but smile. They really were made for each other, and he was glad they'd gotten together.

"You can eat more than one bite of each cake, you know that, right?" Skye laughed as he took a small forkful of the fourth cake and gave it a try.

He wasn't going to be any help deciding which cake they should have at their wedding. They all tasted great.

"I have plans later and don't want to be bouncing off the walls with a sugar high for the rest of the day," he said.

On the other side of the island, Skye rested her forearms on the counter and leaned forward expectantly. "What kind of plans?"

Dane was wondering how much he could say about his date with Lexi before Skye started in on the whole is-it-serious line of questioning. He flat out did not want his sister involved in his sex life—or at least what he hoped might turn into some sex in his life. He wasn't going there.

Before he had a chance to wiggle out from under the question, Jax answered for him. "He's got a date with Lexi Fletcher, the new paramedic at the station house. They're going out to dinner tonight."

Dane's jaw dropped. He hadn't said a word about the date to anyone, so how the hell had Jax found out? Then again, he supposed Lexi could have mentioned it to someone.

"Dude, you work in a firehouse," Jax

said. "There aren't any secrets there. People have been taking bets on when the two of you would go on your first date. You guys have been mooning over each other for a month."

Dane snorted. "I haven't been mooning. I've simply been...interested."

"Okay." Jax shrugged, taking a bite of the cake with lemon filling. "Whatever you say."

Dane would have argued, but Skye interrupted. "Forget about Jax. Tell me about Lexi. What's she like? Where you going to dinner? Do you think she'll want to come to the wedding or will that send the wrong signal? You are thinking long-term here, right?"

Dane stifled a groan. This is exactly why he hadn't wanted to get into this with his sister. She might only ask one question, but it would be in ninety-six parts.

He held up his hands. "Slow down, Skye. Did you miss the part where this is a first date? I don't even know anything about Lexi yet." Other than the fact that she was beautiful and he was attracted as hell to her. "That's why we're going to dinner, so I can learn more about her. I haven't decided where I'm taking her to dinner yet, but it will be someplace nice. As far as everything else, let's not make it out to be anything more than it is yet, okay?"

"But—" Skye started, before he cut her off.

"It's just a date, Skye. If it goes well, maybe we'll go on a second one. That's about as far ahead as I'm thinking."

Skye looked dejected, probably because she'd already been planning what kind of cake she'd make for Dane and Lexi's wedding. Which was hilarious since she couldn't seem to come up with one for her own big day.

Of course, he wasn't being exactly honest with his sister. In reality, he was hoping his date with Lexi went really well. But there was no way he was ever going to tell his sister that.

Dane had known how special Lexi was the second she'd walked into the station that first day at work. Besides being the most attractive woman he'd ever seen, there was something about the confident way she carried herself along with the calm way she did her job that impressed the hell out of him. What could he say? He was a sucker for a strong, confident woman.

If there was ever a woman out there in the world who was perfect for him, it was Lexi.

It wasn't like he didn't date—he wasn't a monk—but there weren't many women who were interested in getting serious with a firefighter. Some thought they were into it, but the first time their new boyfriend walked in smelling like a charcoal briquette, things got too real too fast. They usually bailed after that.

But that obviously wouldn't be a problem with Lexi. She was a paramedic, which was like having a PhD in firefighters. She knew exactly what the job entailed and what she was getting into when she dated one.

He was putting the cart before the horse, though. First, they had to spend time with each other outside of work and see if they were even compatible. If they were, maybe then he'd allow himself to think about something more a little further down the road. But, hey, a man could dream.

"So, have you decided which cake you like best?" Skye asked.

Dane glanced down and realized he'd been eating the entire time he'd been daydreaming about Lexi. He couldn't remember a single thing he'd tasted.

"They're all great," he told his sister. "Why don't you make all of them? That way you wouldn't have to spend so much time worrying about which one is right."

Jax actually looked hopeful at that suggestion, but Skye frowned.

"You've spent the last hour eating cake and the best you can come up with is to make them all?" she demanded. "If you think you're getting out of here after a lame suggestion like that, you can forget it. I don't care if we have to make a hundred cakes, you're not leaving until we have the perfect one for our wedding."

Dane was about to tease her about writing down the cakes' flavors on pieces of paper and picking one out of a hat, but then he saw the look of near panic on his sister's face. Crap, she was really freaking out about this. He took a deep breath and got serious. Skye was his sister, and she needed help.

"Let's take a step back and see if we can trim the list of possibilities down to a more manageable number, okay?" he said gently.

Skye regarded him suspiciously. "How are we going to do that?"

"Simple." He set his fork down and put all the cakes they'd tasted in a row. "Instead of trying to figure which one you like the most, pick the cake you like the least. Jax and I will do the same until we narrow it down to the one that stands out from all the others."

She considered that for a minute then nodded. "Okay, I can do that."

As Skye focused on the cakes, Dane saw Jax mouth a silent *thank you.*

That's what brothers were for, right?

Chapter Three

LEXI WAS PUTTING on her shoes when the doorbell rang. Ignoring her suddenly racing pulse, she finished buckling the straps on her platform heels then forced herself to check her reflection in the mirror before walking out of her bedroom and slowly making her way to the door when all she wanted to do was run.

"Play it cool," she murmured. "Don't let him see how geeked you are. He'll think you've never gone on a date."

Thank goodness Dane hadn't seen her thirty minutes ago when she was running around like a crazy person putting away all the clothes she'd tried on so he wouldn't know she was a complete mess. She'd seriously emptied her whole closet looking for the perfect thing to wear. As usual, she'd ended up going with the first thing she'd tried on. But not without a lot of second-guessing and panic-induced hyperventilation.

Crap, it really was like she hadn't ever

gone on a date.

She'd always been relaxed and confident when it came to dating and hanging out with the opposite sex. Heck, she had to be in her line of work. But, with Dane, that relaxed, confident feeling she was so used to having, seemed to have been lost somewhere in the back of her clothes closet. Maybe it was the fact he was so attractive. Or maybe it was the twinkle in his eyes when he laughed. Then again, maybe it was the fact she'd already seen him without his shirt. Whatever it was, the thought of spending the entire evening with him had her as giddy as a teenager. Probably because she really wanted this to work out with Dane. The guy—at least what she knew of him—seemed perfect in every way possible.

When she got to the door, she stopped to take a deep breath, wishing once again that Melinda was here to help keep her calm. But her roommate had to cover a double shift in the ER, so Lexi was on her own.

Showtime.

Lexi peeked through the peephole to make sure it was really Dane then took another deep breath and swung it open wide. For a moment, all she could do was stare. Damn, Dane looked even yummier than he did at the station. And that was saying something because he took the DF&R uniform to another whole level. But in faded jeans, loose casual button-down, and a little scruff on his jawline, he looked good enough to eat.

She had a naughty thought about skipping dinner out and eating at her place instead, followed by dessert in bed, but told herself to chill out. It was way too early for anything like that.

Realizing she was staring, Lexi smiled. "Gotta love a man who's on time." She opened the door wider. "Come on in."

Lexi couldn't miss the sexy-as-sin cologne that mingled so deliciously with his own masculine scent as he entered the apartment. She had to resist the urge to step over and bury her face in the curve of his neck.

He turned to her as she closed the door, completely oblivious to her sudden interest in his scent. "I ran into your roommate, Melinda, when I stopped by the hospital today to visit Wayne. She gave me the third degree about my intentions toward you and a lecture on safe sex."

Lexi groaned, knowing the answer to the question before she even asked it. "She didn't really do that, did she?"

"Oh yeah." Dane chuckled. "But don't worry, I completely get it. She's a friend and wants to make sure you're not going out with a dirtbag. I must have passed inspection because she went out of her way to make sure I knew she wouldn't be home until late."

Lexi could imagine her roommate giving Dane a conspiratorial wink. "Melinda's a lot of things, but subtle isn't one of them."

Dane's mouth quirked. "Yeah, I picked

up on that."

She gave Dane a quick tour of the apartment she shared with her best friend. It didn't take long since it wasn't that big. But a two-bedroom, two-bath apartment with an eat-in kitchen and small living room was enough for her and Melinda. They both spent more time at work than at home, so it didn't make sense to spend a lot of money on a bigger place.

"How's Wayne doing?" she asked as she showed off her bedroom. And yeah, she noticed him checking out the bed, though whether he was checking to see if they would both fit on it, or simply looking for bondage gear, she wasn't sure.

"He's doing well, all things considered," he told her as they headed back for the living room. "He still has a headache from that concussion, but, overall, he's in good spirits, even though his apartment and most of his possessions are gone. He was really grateful to get the clothes and the other stuff I brought him."

She picked up her purse from the couch. "Most of his possessions? Were Jax and the others able to save anything from his place at all?"

Dane shook his head. "Not much. A couple books, a photo album, and a small lockbox full of papers. I told him we'd hold onto the stuff for him at the station so he doesn't have to worry about it."

"Is there anything else he needs?" she

asked as they headed for the door, thinking she could stop by and bring the man some more stuff tomorrow.

"I don't think so," Dane said. "I think he needs friends a lot more than he needs stuff. I ended up spending nearly three hours with him today. I barely made it out of there in time to go home and get changed so I could make it here on time to pick you up."

They took the stairs down to the parking lot and Dane's white Ford F150 pickup truck. As he helped her into the vehicle, Lexi couldn't help thinking about how awesome it was that Dane had taken his off-time to sit with a man they'd rescued. It wasn't something everyone would do. Yet one more thing to like about Dane.

As Dane drove, they chatted a bit more about Wayne, but also about all the other people they helped on an almost daily basis in their jobs. She was struck by how many names Dane seemed to remember from his calls. He laughed and talked about them like they were family. It was pretty amazing...and inspiring.

She'd expected Dane to take her to a traditional steak restaurant, or maybe a barbecue place—either of which would have been fine with her—so she was surprised when they pulled up in front of a place with an obvious Southwest feel to it. The building made her think of a Mexican hacienda, complete with arching windows and ivy vining all along the front of it.

"I guess I should have asked before we got here," he said. "But are you okay with Mexican?"

She smiled. "Love it."

"Good. I've eaten at this place a couple of times, and the food is really good," he said when he came around to open her door. "It's also quiet enough that we can still talk without having to shout."

The interior of the restaurant matched the outside with lots of wood, brick, and low lighting. And the aroma coming from the kitchen was delicious. There weren't a lot of people around, but that was probably normal for a Thursday night. Some people might feel weird going out on a date in the middle of the week like this, but when you worked twenty-four hours on and forty-eight off, you got used to having weekends twice a week and going out for dinner whenever you could.

When Dane asked for a quiet booth somewhere in the back, the hostess gave them a knowing smile and said she had the perfect table. Lexi hadn't sat in a booth on a date with a guy since she was a teenager, but as Dane slid into the curved seat beside her, she remembered why she liked it. It was sexy to sit so close to a guy their hips and thighs touched.

Lexi looked around the restaurant as she sipped her sangria. "How did you find this place?"

"It was one night after I pulled a partial on another shift." Dane tipped back his bottle of beer, taking a long drink. "We had a big residential fire that night, and everything ran late. Considering I hadn't slept in twenty-four hours, I probably should have gone straight home and collapsed into bed, but I was too wired. I was driving around burning off extra energy when I saw this place. Maybe it was simply the adrenaline from the fire, or maybe it was because I hadn't eaten in twelve hours, but whatever the reason, it was one of the best meals I've ever had. Since then, I come here at least once a week."

"Do you cover other people's shifts for them a lot?"

"Sometimes." He shrugged. "I love the job and I figured out a long time ago that I don't need as much sleep as other people, so I pull extra shifts now and then, especially for the married firefighters."

Yet another thing about Dane that was special. Seriously, could she find a better guy? He was like a saint—with washboard abs.

Lexi opened her mouth to commend him for pulling extra shifts for the married firefighters, but their server showed up at their table to take their orders. Crap, she hadn't even looked at her menu.

"What do you recommend?" she asked Dane.

"Their soft shell beef and chicken burritos are their signature dish, so you can't go wrong with those. Usually, I get one of each when I order them."

Lexi handed the server her menu with a smile. "Exactly what he said."

"Make that two," Dane said, handing the woman his menu, too.

Their server laughed and jotted something down on her order pad. "I do like people who know what they want."

After the woman left, Lexi caught Dane regarding her out of the corner of her eye, blatant interest on his face. Like he knew exactly what he wanted—and it had nothing to do with food.

"So," she said softly, trying not to think too much about how close they were sitting to each other, or how nice his leg felt pressed up against her. "How long have you been a firefighter, and have you been at Station 58 the whole time?"

Dane's mouth curved into a sexy little smile, making her wonder if he was aware of how easily he put her off balance. Hopefully not. She was doing her best to come off cool and casual. She picked up her glass and was surprised to see her hand shaking a little. What the heck was it about this guy that had her so spun up?

She took her time sipping her drink, praying she didn't spill it. That would be perfect.

He took another swig of beer before answering. "I joined DF&R a couple months out of high school. I was one of the youngest recruits at the fire academy and wasn't even twenty by the time I came off of probationary status. Stewart had pull even back then and got me assigned to the five-eight. I've been there ever since—almost fourteen years."

Lexi blinked. In her experience, very few people walked right out of high school and into the fire academy. The firefighting profession was something of a calling, and most of the firefighters she knew had spent a few years doing other things—college, the military, even odd jobs—before they realized what they wanted to do with their life. For someone Dane's age to have fourteen years of experience was unusual.

"Do you come from a family of firefighters?" she asked.

She figured that had to be the case, since it was about the only thing that would explain joining the department at such a young age. But Dane shook his head.

"No, nothing like that," he said quietly, rubbing his thumb absently back and forth over the label on his beer bottle.

The way he said the words made her think he'd rather not get into the reasons he'd become a firefighter, and she felt like crap for bringing it up.

She reached out and placed her hand on top of his much larger one, giving it a squeeze. "It's okay. We don't have to talk about it if you don't want to."

He frowned, clearly struggling with the decision. She got the sense that while part of Dane wanted to tell her about it, the other part didn't want to relive whatever it was.

Before either of them could say anything else, their server showed up with two plates of tortilla wrapped goodness smothered in melted cheese. Lexi was forced to slide over a little so she wouldn't poke Dane with her elbows as she cut her burritos. She immediately missed the warmth of his body and found herself scooting closer again when she was done.

"It was the summer after I graduated from high school," Dane said suddenly. He was staring down at his plate, lost in memories of a time long ago. "I was heading to Texas A&M in the fall and decided to take the summer off so I could hang out with my friends before going to college. I was down in the bonus room in my parents' house, playing video games when the fire started."

Lexi's stomach clenched. She already knew how this was going to end.

"I thought my mom had burned something in the oven, so I didn't pay attention. I didn't know the house was on fire until it was too late. The wiring was faulty and..." He swallowed hard, still not looking at her. "By the time I ran up to the first floor, it was engulfed in flames. I couldn't get upstairs to my parents' room, so I shouted as loud as I could then ran outside, sure they were right behind me. I was young and stupid and didn't know any of the stuff about fire that I know now. I couldn't save them."

Lexi blinked back tears. "What happened wasn't your fault, Dane."

He nodded, clearing his throat. "I know that now."

"So instead of going to college, you became a firefighter."

"Yeah." He sighed. "I blamed myself for my parents' death. Becoming a firefighter and saving others was my way to make things right."

The knowledge that Dane had carried the weight of his parents' death since he was eighteen broke Lexi's heart.

"Did it?" she asked softly.

"I've gotten to the point where I realize there was nothing I could have done for my parents even if I'd had the training and the equipment with me at the time," he admitted. "Now, I simply do what I do hoping to keep another kid out there from losing their parents like I did."

Lexi wiped a stray tear away from her cheek. "I have no doubt you've done that for a lot more than one kid."

"I like to think so." He looked at her, his mouth edging up. "Enough about me and my depressing past. How about you? Do you come from a family of paramedics?"

Despite how heavy the conversation had been, Lexi couldn't help laughing. "In the category of the world being a really small place after all, I enrolled at Texas A&M, too."

"Seriously?" Dane scooped up a forkful of beef burrito. "You're an Aggie? What was your major?"

She finished chewing before she

answered. Dane was right. The food was delicious. "I was planning to go to medical school, so my major was biomedical science."

Dane did a double take. "You were going to be a doctor? Not that I'm complaining you decided to become a paramedic instead, since I got to meet you, but how the heck did that happen?"

She waved her fork. "College advisors are constantly on pre-med students to do activities outside the school environment to improve their resume for medical school. For me, that activity turned out to be EMT work. During the summer semester of my sophomore year, I completed an intensive nineteen-day training course to get certified as an EMT-Basic then took the Registry Exam so I could work with DF&R during the summers of my junior and senior years."

"Wow. That sounds like an insane workload. I can't believe you didn't burn out."

She shrugged. "I was young, and it was all about getting into medical school, which is what I always wanted. Or at least, that's what I thought I wanted. But getting to ride on a rescue truck gave me a chance to see and do things I never would have otherwise. Not only did I realize I liked being a first responder, I also figured out I'd glamorized the work doctors did every day. As an EMS worker, I got to know a lot of doctors and nurses from the hospitals, especially those who work in the ERs. They were brutally honest about what they liked and didn't like about the profession. It helped me see things differently."

He glanced at her as he started in on his chicken burrito. "So you decided to not go to medical school?"

She nodded. "In the end, I realized I'd rather do a job I liked, even if I made less money doing it, than to do a job I disliked, where I made more."

"I can't argue with that."

"My mom and dad weren't as thrilled with my decision," she said. "They were over the moon about having a doctor in the family. More than anything, though, they wanted me to be happy." She sipped her wine. "Luckily, all that pre-med made it easy to get licensed as a full paramedic, and the work I did during the two previous summers was enough to get me hired full-time at DF&R right away."

Dane picked up his beer. "I'm guessing you still get a lot of people calling you crazy for walking away from the chance to be a doctor and make all that money, huh?"

She smiled. "A few people. But I usually don't value their opinion very much, so I rarely listen to them."

"I'm glad to hear that. Because I have it on good authority it's always better to go with your heart on stuff like this and ignore people who try to convince you otherwise."

"What do you mean?"

"My sister, Skye, used to work on Wall Street making butt loads of money. She walked away from it all for a chance to move back to Dallas and bake cupcakes. I thought she was out of her mind and told her so. She promptly told me what I could do with that opinion." He finished the last of his burritos. "It's a long story, but ultimately it turned out that she was right, and I've learned my lesson about following your heart."

Lexi laughed. "She sounds like someone I'd like to meet."

"She usually stops by the station regularly, but since she and Jax are getting married next week, she's been too busy with the wedding. She's already said she wants to meet you, too."

Lexi lifted a brow. "You told her about us?"

Dane chuckled. "I didn't have to. According to Jax, everyone in the station already knows. Apparently, our coworkers noticed something going on between us before either of us did."

Lexi supposed she could believe that. She'd gone out of her way to ask the other female firefighters and paramedics at the station about Dane's relationship status before transferring.

Dane pushed away his empty plate then rested his arm on top of the booth in back of her. "By the way, there's something I've been wanting to ask you."

She wiggled a little closer, resting her hand on his jean-clad thigh and tilting her head to look at him. "What's that?"

He returned her gaze, his dark eyes

curious. "You'd been working at Station 44 since joining DF&R, right? What made you decide to come to the five-eight?"

Lexi felt her face heat. Okay, how was she going to get out of this one? It probably wasn't a good out idea to come out and admit to stalking him. Then again, he might already have a pretty good idea why she'd requested a transfer, so she didn't want him to catch her in a fib.

"Oh, I don't know." She shrugged. "I heard there were a lot of interesting things to see and do at Station 58. I decided to follow my heart and go for it."

Dane moved his arm from the back of the booth, draping it across her shoulders, a smile tipping up the corners of his mouth. "Well, whatever your reasons, count me among those who are glad you did."

Lexi was pretty sure Dane had figured out his presence at Station 58 had been one of the factors in transferring there. She appreciated the fact he didn't call her on it, though.

"So, is it official?" he asked.

She flexed her hand, squeezing his thigh. It wasn't her fault. Thighs as muscular as Dane's were made to be squeezed. She was certain there was a law written about that somewhere. She was still considering the wording of a law like that when she figured out that she had no idea what he'd asked her. What was official?

"What's that?"

"Are we dating now?" he asked, a teasing glint in his eyes.

"Possibly," she said. "I suppose it depends on how well the rest of the evening goes."

Dane leaned in a little closer, and Lexi thought for one wild second he was going to kiss her. Instead, he grinned, flashing her those sexy dimples.

"Then I guess I'll have to make sure the rest of the date goes well, won't I?" he said softly.

With his mouth mere inches from hers, the urge to pull his head down the rest of the way for a kiss was practically impossible to resist, but, somehow, she did. "I don't think you have to work too hard. It's going really well so far."

His eyes turned molten. "And to think, it's only getting started."

Lexi would have kissed him for sure then, but their server chose that exact moment to show up and ask if they wanted dessert.

Dane didn't take his smoldering gaze off Lexi. "I'd absolutely love dessert."

Butterflies fluttered in her tummy. Something told her Dane wasn't talking about the Kahlua cake on the restaurant menu.

Chapter Four

DANE SIGHED AS he pulled up in front of Cowboys Red River dance hall. He would much rather have headed back to his apartment, or Lexi's, or anyplace private enough to let them get horizontal. Hell, who was he kidding? He would have been satisfied with a broom closet big enough for the two of them to stand up in. Anywhere they could make out...and do other things.

He told himself to behave. Tonight wasn't about getting Lexi into bed as fast as he could. It was about showing her the best night of her life. Call it delayed gratification, but he figured that if he played his cards right, he'd be getting to spend a lot more than one night with her.

But, damn, he was having one hell of a hard time keeping that thought locked in his head when all he really wanted to do at that moment was pull Lexi into his arms and kiss her until her dress melted off.

Dane threw the truck in park and took a deep breath, telling his hard-on to shut up and stop trying to drive.

He wasn't sure what was going on with him tonight. He'd never had a problem keeping his cool around a woman. But there was something about Lexi that drove him insane. It could be the way she looked so hot in that sexy little black dress that showed off her legs, not to mention some seriously dangerous curves. Then again, maybe it was the tantalizing perfume she was wearing that made him want to bury his face in her long, dark hair and stay there the rest of the night.

Hell, it might have been the casual way she'd rested her hand on his thigh back at the restaurant. At first, he wasn't sure she'd even realized what she was doing to him. But then he'd caught the gleam in her eye as she sat there squeezing his leg in pulsing rhythm with his heartbeat. That's when he knew Lexi was perfectly aware of how much she was turning him on. She was teasing the hell out of him, and enjoying herself as she did it.

"I've been here before," Lexi said when he opened the passenger door for her. "With the crew from my old station. They usually have great bands here."

He locked the truck then took her hand. "Do you like to dance?"

She smiled. "Definitely! What about you?"

He grinned. "I've been known to two-step on occasion."

"And is tonight one of those occasions?"

"It is."

Her smile broadened. "Good. Then let's go dance!"

Dane chuckled as she gave his hand a tug. He was starting to wonder if she approached everything she did with as much enthusiasm as she did dancing. Of course, that immediately made him think about doing a completely different physical activity with her. His cock hardened again. Damn, he'd finally gotten the thing to behave. How the hell was he going to dance now?

Lexi didn't give him a chance to worry too much about it as she dragged him through the door so fast he barely had time to slow down and pay the cover charge. Once inside, Lexi made a beeline for the huge dance floor. The band on stage was playing a popular country song, and he and Lexi easily slipped into the flow of people and started two-stepping around the floor.

He quickly figured out Lexi was one hell of a good dancer. Before long, they were scooting, spinning, and shuffling around the floor like they'd been dancing together for years. The music was too loud to even consider talking, so Dane made do with gazing into her beautiful blue eyes.

The band played one great song after another, so he and Lexi stayed on the floor along with everyone else. Dane had no idea how long they danced, but at some point he looked up and realized the place was a lot more crowded, making it harder to get around the doughnut-shaped floor. Then the band switched gears, playing a much slower tune and calling all the couples out for a little slow dancing.

Lexi slipped into his arms as if she belonged there, which he was beginning to think she most certainly did. He slid his right hand behind her back, pulling her close, then casually rested his palm on the upper curve of her ass, letting his fingers trace little circles on the sensitive spot right at the base of her spine. She shivered the slightest bit before resting her cheek against his chest.

He groaned at how good Lexi felt nestled up against him, but he doubted she could hear over the music. There was no way she could miss the hard-on he sported in his jeans, though. Hell, the thing was pressing right up against her belly begging for attention. Lexi snuggled even closer, one of her hands digging into the muscles of his shoulder like she wasn't ever going to let him move away. She didn't have to worry about that. He wasn't going anywhere.

When the song came to an end—way too fast, in his opinion—Lexi tipped her head back to look up at him. Seeing the hunger in her eyes, and knowing it almost certainly matched the look in his own, Dane did the only thing he could. He dipped his head and kissed her.

He swore he felt a spark jump between them when their lips touched. He was also pretty sure he heard Lexi moan against his mouth. Then again, that might have been him groaning. It was hard to tell.

He buried his free hand in her hair, cradling her head as he traced his tongue around her lips. She parted them, inviting him in, and he slipped his tongue into her mouth to two-step with hers. Damn, she tasted good! It was all he could do to control himself.

From the way Lexi was clutching the front of his shirt and kissing him back, he wasn't the only one having problems keeping things PG-rated.

Dane didn't realize the band had started playing again, or that the other people on the dance floor were moving around him and Lexi like a tide until someone bumped into him. Grabbing Lexi's hand, he led her through the crowd and off the floor. After a kiss like that, dancing was the last thing he wanted to do.

He headed for one of the bars so they could grab a couple of drinks. Besides the fact that they had been dancing for a while and she was probably as thirsty as he was, he needed something else to focus on. If he didn't calm down before they left, he was probably going to rush into something, and he didn't want to do that. Not with someone this amazing.

When he ordered two bottles of water, the bartender looked at him like he had horns growing out of his head. He guessed water wasn't a big seller around here.

Dane handed one to Lexi to see her regarding him with an expression half amused, half hungry...and altogether sexy. This woman was dangerous all right.

He drained half the bottle of water in one gulp. When he looked at Lexi again, she'd turned her attention to the mechanical bull pit set up along one of the walls near the pool tables.

"Have you ridden the bull here before?" he asked.

Now she was looking at him like he had horns growing out of his head. "Are you crazy? I'm a paramedic. I've seen people screw themselves up royally falling off a curb. There's no way in hell you'll get me on that thing."

He chuckled. "Oh, come on, it's not that bad. They're not nearly as hard to ride as the real thing. The operator will put the thing on slow if you tell him you're a newbie."

Lexi's eyes widened. "You've ridden real bulls?"

He nodded. "I've ridden in quite a few rodeos, including some charity DF&R events. Trust me when I say mechanical bulls are easier."

She eyed the mechanical contraption doubtfully, but Dane could see curiosity warring with her better judgement.

"I'd never be able to stay on that thing, no matter how slowly it was moving," she said.

He swigged some water. "If you want to

give it a go, you could always ride with me."

Lexi blinked. "We can do that? I mean, they'd let us?"

"Sure. They don't care."

She still seemed doubtful, but finally nodded. "I'll be mad at myself tomorrow if I don't, so let's do this." She gave him a stern look. "But if we fall off and get hurt, you're going to be the one to explain to Captain Stewart how it happened."

Dane chuckled. "Deal. But don't worry. If we fall off, I'll make sure you come down on top of me so you don't get hurt."

There were three women waiting in line to ride ahead of them, but they all chickened out. For a second, Dane thought Lexi was going to bail, too, but she took a deep breath, kicked off her shoes, and stomped across the squishy mats.

Dane handed the operator a twenty. "There's another twenty in it if you don't kill us."

The man nodded his head and tipped his beat-up cowboy hat. Dane figured that was about as good as he was going to get.

The thing didn't look much like a bull but more like something you'd see on a carousel—if it was a demented carousel for really disturbed kids. The body was a basic barrel shape with no legs and a barely recognizable head with floppy ears instead of horns. But there was a simple saddle to sit on, with a wide strap at the top to hold onto.

"How the heck do I even get on this

thing?" she asked, staring at the high back in alarm.

Dane could have suggested several different ways, but finally decided to reach out and pick her up by the waist, sitting her on the forward part of the saddle.

She smiled at him. "Thanks."

Lexi adjusted her dress, pulling it up a bit here and there to get comfortable, flashing a lot of thigh in the process. Damn, she had nice legs.

Dane hopped up behind her before he could think too much about her legs—and what it would feel like if they were wrapped around him instead of a stupid fake bull. Riding a mechanical bull with a hard-on might or might not be legal in Texas—it was a weird state like that—but it wouldn't be very comfortable.

He reached past her hip and grabbed the strap positioned between her legs. He really had to think hard about what he was doing so the fact that his hand was inches from her pussy didn't distract him too much.

Wrapping his free hand around her, he pulled her even more tightly against him, which made the junction of her thighs press enticingly against the hand he was using to hold onto the strap and his hard-on nestle temptingly against her ass. The hard-on he wasn't supposed to have at the moment—yeah, that one.

"I think I understand why you wanted to ride this thing," she murmured over her shoulder. "It definitely has the potential to be interesting."

That was an understatement if he'd ever heard one.

"Ready?" the operator called.

Dane nodded at the man, and the bull began to move.

Riding a bull, whether a real one or a mechanical beast, wasn't about guessing what the creature would do. It wasn't even about holding on tight. It was about relaxing and feeling the flow of the movement.

At first, Lexi was stiff as a board, trying to clench her legs tight to the bull's sides like she thought that would keep her on the thing. It wouldn't, but she didn't know that. Dane kept his body loose and balanced, holding on for the both of them and hoping she relaxed enough to enjoy this.

She did, shocking him at how quickly she got into the bull's rhythm and began moving as one with him.

The bull operator earned his money, setting up a routine of mostly simple turns and rolling waves with enough change of direction to keep it interesting. It was the slow, ocean-like wave motion that got to Dane first, as Lexi's ass began to move against his hard-on in the most erotic motion. There was no way Lexi wasn't feeling the hard shaft of his cock moving against her ass, because he sure as hell was.

Beneath the arm he had wrapped around her, Dane felt her muscles tense and relax as she began to gyrate, riding him as much as she was riding the bull. But it was when she started grinding against the hand holding the bull's harness strap that he really lost it.

Fortunately, the operator chose that moment for a sudden change of direction, combined with a sharp flip of the bull's back end. The move tossed Dane right off, and he took Lexi with him.

He twisted in the air as he fell, making sure he came down on his back with her on top of him. It wasn't exactly the most comfortable landing in the world, especially when Lexi's hip slammed into his stomach. But considering he ended up flat on his back with a beautiful woman sprawled across his chest, he could put up with the minor pain.

"That was more fun that I thought it'd be," she said in a deep, husky voice.

He ran his hand down her back, making her arch against him like a kitty. "I don't think I was expecting that either."

She leaned closer, her mouth about to come down on his when Dane noticed a pair of booted feet on the mat next to his head.

"Y'all okay?" the mechanical bull operator asked, his voice full of concern. "Y'all need a paramedic or something?"

Lexi smiled, her perfect, full lips only inches from his own.

Dane chuckled. "That's okay. I already found the only paramedic I need."

Chapter Five

LEXI DIDN'T REALIZE she was still sitting in her car in the parking lot of the hospital staring off into the distance—probably with a very goofy grin on her face—until Melinda texted asking where she was. Crap, she was supposed to meet her friend for lunch fifteen minutes ago.

It wasn't her fault. She couldn't be blamed for wanting to relive last night's date with Dane. It had been pretty awesome. In fact, she was certain it was going to go down as one of the very best dates of her life. She couldn't even say which part of the evening had been her favorite.

Dane had picked a great place for dinner, but while the food had been amazing, the conversation had been even better. She couldn't remember when she'd had so much fun getting to know a guy. He'd been so easy to talk to, and considering the kind of personal stuff he'd gotten into, it seemed obvious he was comfortable with her as well. If they hadn't done anything else last night but talk, she would have been fine with that.

But to say they *had* done something else last night was an understatement. The entire evening at the club had been amazing. The kiss they'd shared on the dance floor had about lit her on fire. She'd already been a little aroused from the flirting during dinner, and dancing with Dane had only gotten her hotter. If he hadn't dragged her off the dance floor when he did, she might not have been responsible for what happened next.

But, truthfully, as turned on as she'd gotten from that, it paled in comparison to what they'd done on the bull. She only prayed it didn't show up on YouTube because they'd come damn close to having sex right there on that mechanical testament to humanity's lack of intelligence.

At first, she'd been too nervous at the prospect of getting tossed off the thing to consider how sexual their position on the bull really was. But then Dane had wrapped his strong arms around her, positioning one hand between her legs while his hard cock had pressed up against her bottom. That's when she figured out things were about to get a little naughty

Okay, maybe a *lot* naughty. Without a doubt, what they'd done on that bull had been the sexiest thing ever. She hadn't merely gotten excited, aroused, and wet as hell. If they hadn't fallen off when they had, she was thoroughly convinced she would have climaxed at some point.

Orgasm by mechanical bull—that would definitely have been a first for her. Okay, she was born and bred in Texas, and that still sounded wrong.

She'd been a little dazed during the drive back to her place, but Dane hadn't seemed to mind. He'd tugged her across the bench seat of his pickup truck and snuggled her close. That was when Lexi knew they had something really good going on. If you could sit in comfortable silence with a guy for that long and not feel the urge to fill it with meaningless chitchat, then he was definitely a keeper.

Dane had been the perfect gentleman when they'd gotten back to her place, walking Lexi all the way to her apartment and making sure she got in okay. While he'd been telling her he had a great time and was looking forward to going out with her again, she'd pulled him inside for a good night kiss. No way in hell was she letting him get away without one—not after he'd gotten her so fired up.

That good night kiss had turned into a twenty minute make out session against the wall by the front door, and it had taken all her control to keep from dragging him off to her bedroom. The man could kiss like nobody's business!

Before he'd left, they'd set up another date for Sunday, their next day off. Lexi had to work hard to convince herself she could hold out that long. Yeah, she'd see him at work on Saturday, but that was different. At work, she'd have to be on her best behavior. That meant no kissing on top of the fire truck—or anywhere else for that matter.

After sending Melinda a quick text to let her know she was there, Lexi reached into the backseat to grab the bag of books and magazines she'd brought for Wayne. Since she was meeting Melinda for lunch anyway, she figured she'd stop by and visit the older man while she was there.

Lexi waved at a few of the doctors and nurses she knew as she made her way to the nurse's station in the ER. Melinda wasn't there yet, so Lexi asked the nurse at the desk if she knew what room Wayne was in. Since his injuries were minor, she doubted they'd left him in one of the urgent care rooms. She only hoped they hadn't already released him.

The nurse at the desk was still checking which room Wayne was in when Melinda's voice interrupted them.

"You don't need to do that, Kim. I got it."

Lexi turned and gave her roommate a smile. Melinda had worked late last night then come in early this morning. It was barely noon, and she already looked exhausted.

"Hey," Lexi said. "I brought some books and magazines for Wayne to read. I thought I'd drop them off before we grab lunch."

Melinda didn't return her smile. For some reason, Lexi suddenly got a funny feeling in her stomach. She wasn't sure what her friend's silence meant, but she didn't like it.

"What is it?" she asked.

Melinda shook her head. "I'm sorry. Wayne didn't make it."

Lexi stared, sure she hadn't heard right. "Wait...what?"

"Wayne passed away during the night." Melinda sighed. "I think it was his heart."

Tears stung Lexi's eyes. She blinked them back, stunned by her reaction to Wayne's death. She'd been doing this job for a long time. Although losing patients was always hard, she'd gotten used to it. But Wayne was different. He wasn't supposed to die.

"How is that even possible?" she demanded. "Dane stopped to see Wayne yesterday and said he was fine. They talked for hours."

Tears trickled down her face. She tried to dash them away so no one would see. She was a paramedic, dammit. Paramedics weren't supposed to cry.

"Melinda, is everything okay?"

Lexi turned and saw a middle-aged man in a white lab coat approaching them, a concerned look on his friendly face. She recognized him as the doctor the news crew had been interviewing the other day about the kid who'd saved his family from a fire.

"Lexi, this is Dr. Lambert. He's the

attending physician in charge of our residents. Doctor, Lexi Fletcher, a paramedic at one of the local fire stations." Melinda's smile was sad. "She's the one who brought in Wayne Moore."

Dr. Lambert nodded. "I'm sorry about Mr. Moore. Was he a friend?"

Lexi shook her head, tears threatening to flow again. Crap. "No. I'd never met him before bringing him in the other night."

Whether she wanted them to or not, the tears made another appearance. She wiped them away with the heel of her hand. She wasn't sure why Wayne's death was hitting her so hard.

Dr. Lambert gave her an understanding smile. "It's okay. You don't have to try to hide the fact that you have a heart and care about the people you rescue. I only talked to Mr. Moore once while I was taking a group of residents on a rotation, but he seemed like a very nice man. Someone should mourn the loss of a person like that."

Lexi nodded, not trusting herself to speak right then. She could see why the hospital had put Dr. Lambert in charge of training the next generation of doctors. He clearly cared about the people he'd taken an oath to heal.

"How could this have happened?" she asked, wondering if she and Trent had missed something when they'd treated Wayne. "His pulse and blood pressure were slightly elevated when my partner and I brought him in, but nothing serious."

Dr. Lambert shook his head. "There was nothing in any of the initial screening work that indicated a problem either. It was a surprise to us when Mr. Moore's heart gave out during the night, but he was in his seventies, so it isn't unusual. Especially after what he'd been through. The stress of the fire, the concussion, and his anxiety over what he was going to do next now that his home was gone were probably too much for him."

Lexi frowned. "Wayne couldn't be revived?"

"Unfortunately, no. Dr. Patton did everything he could, but he couldn't save him."

Lexi sighed. Poor Wayne had no one in his life to miss him or mourn him, except for them. It made Lexi realize more than ever the importance of friends and family, and about surrounding yourself with people you loved and who loved you in return. The time she and Dane had spent together last night seemed even more special.

Chapter Six

I'VE NEVER GONE paddleboarding before," Lexi said. "Is it difficult to learn?"

Dane glanced at her as he took the exit for Lake Carolyn, letting his gaze linger on her bare legs before turning his attention to the road again. The shorts and tank top she wore revealed a lot more skin than they concealed, and the sight was doing a number on him for sure. Not that he was complaining. The biggest reason he'd suggested going paddleboarding was so he could see Lexi in a bikini.

"I don't think so. I've never done it either." He grinned as he turned into the parking lot. "That's why I signed us up for a class and a guided tour of the lake."

"Good thinking." She smiled. "Now I have to hope I don't make an idiot of myself."

Dane pulled into a space and cut the engine. "I've seen you doing yoga in the gym at the station. You're too graceful ever to make an idiot of yourself."

Lexi unbuckled her seatbelt and leaned closer, one hand on the bench seat between them. "So, you've been watching me, huh?"

"Every chance I get. In a completely non-stalker kind of way, of course." He kissed her. "Come on before I say the hell with paddleboarding and spend the rest of the day right here making out with you."

She was still laughing as he got out of the truck and came around to her side to open the door for her.

"It might be easier if we leave our clothes and stuff in the truck," he suggested.

Lexi nodded, pulling her tank top over her head then skimming off her shorts.

Dane's breath hitched. *Damn.* With her toned body, healthy curves, and long, sexy legs, she looked good enough to eat.

He yanked off his shirt then they sprayed each other down with sunscreen and headed for the board rental place located right on the Mandalay Canal. As they walked, he let Lexi move ahead of him a little bit so he could enjoy the view. And man, what a view. The woman had a spectacular ass. Of course, he'd already discovered that in the best way possible while riding that mechanical bull Thursday evening.

He'd slept in on Friday then lay in bed for another hour thinking about their date the night before. He'd never been with anyone like Lexi. She was easy to talk to and fun to be around, and the moment he'd left her apartment, he couldn't wait to see her again. In fact, he'd been contemplating calling to see if she wanted to do dinner and a movie when she'd called and told him about Wayne. Suggesting doing something frivolous hadn't seemed right after that.

As a firefighter, Dane had to deal with death sometimes. More in car accidents than in fires, but it was all bad. He still couldn't believe the old guy hadn't made it. He'd seemed completely fine when Dane had visited him earlier that day. It made him appreciate life even more.

Things at the station had been interesting on Saturday. Everyone there had known he and Lexi had gone out and demanded details about their date. It was like they were back in high school. Calls had started coming in soon enough, though, and their coworkers forgot all about their date. It had been a tough day on the highways yesterday. Three car accidents caused by some A-holes out street racing in weekend traffic. It was lucky no one had gotten killed.

Dane was still thinking about that when he and Lexi joined the dozen other people who were there to paddleboard. The lessons turned out to be a good idea. Dane had never realized there was so much technique to the whole thing, but they spent forty-five minutes learning how to mount the board, stand up, balance on the water—that was more interesting than he would have thought—

paddle the board the right way, different ways to turn, and finally, how to fall off the board properly then get back on.

Admittedly, he spent most of that time watching Lexi. Like he'd thought, she was a natural when it came to keeping her balance. The way the muscles in her legs flexed as she moved was a thing of beauty.

After the lessons, the guides led them into the canal then let everyone move at their own pace. Dane and Lexi hung back from the rest of the group, slowly paddling past the shops, tourist attractions, walkways, and waterfalls.

"I've been down here a dozen times, but it looks completely different from out on the water. It's beautiful." Lexi smiled at him. "Thanks for thinking of this."

"I've always wanted to do it," he admitted. "Just never found the right person to do it with."

Dane couldn't be sure, but he thought he saw her blush.

"You sure this wasn't an excuse to see me half naked?" she teased.

He chuckled, admiring the way her abs rippled as she paddled her board. "You caught me. Seeing you in a bikini was all part of my devious plan."

"You are so bad," she laughed.

Dane paddled up beside her and leaned over for a kiss. "Maybe a little."

Dane was disappointed when the guides turned everyone around and headed back to the dock. He could have stayed out there with Lexi the whole day.

"We should come back and do one of their sunset paddles," Lexi said as if reading his mind. "Or maybe rent the boards ourselves. What do you think?"

"I think it sounds like a plan," Dane said, leaning over to kiss her again.

* * * * *

When they got back to shore, Lexi and Dane changed out of their swimsuits and into the extra clothes they'd brought with them. For her that meant slipping back into her shorts and tank top—minus the bikini this time—while Dane came out of the changing room wearing cargo shorts and a T-shirt. She didn't mind the cargoes because they still showed off his muscular legs, but she was a little bummed he'd put on a T-shirt. She'd enjoyed seeing those washboard abs of his ripple and flex while he'd worked it on that board.

"You feel like stopping by Keller's Drive-In for burgers then taking them back to my place and eating there?" Dane asked.

Lexi was all about that. She'd never been to Keller's, but everyone she knew raved about their burgers being the best in Dallas. And after basking in the hot, hunky firefighter that was Dane Chandler all day, she definitely wouldn't mind having him all to herself. She was kind of curious to see where he lived, too.

She smiled. "Sounds good to me."

Keller's was a few miles from the paddleboarding place, so it took barely ten minutes to get there. Lexi glanced at Dane as he pulled into one of the drive-in spaces.

"How did you find this place?" she asked. "Another late night shift at the station?"

He chuckled. "Pretty much. We've stopped here a couple times in Engine 58 on the way back from a call."

Lexi ordered a cheeseburger with all the standard fixings while Dane got a double meat with chili and cheese. They both got fries, plus an order of onion rings to share between them as well as chocolate shakes. Because if you went to a drive-in, you had to get shakes. Everything smelled so delicious, she couldn't resist stealing a fry or two on the way to Dane's apartment.

"I've been dying to see where you live," Lexi said as they took the elevator up to the eighth floor of his apartment building.

Dane waited for her to step into the hallway before following her out of the elevator. "It's kind of small and not nearly as nice as your place."

She laughed. "My place is only nice because there are two of us paying the rent."

Dane hadn't been exaggerating when he said his one-bedroom apartment was small. But it was neat and clean and had a big window in the living room with a killer view that made it seem bigger than it really was.

While Dane went into the kitchen to grab some plates, she lingered in the living room to check out the framed photos on the walls. There were some of him with a dark-haired woman with eyes so similar to Dane's she could only be his sister, which meant the middle-aged couple in the pictures must be his parents. All the other photos were of him with the firefighters and paramedics from Station 58. Besides the regular cookouts, there were a few from the various charity and sporting events as well.

"You're really close to the crew at the station, aren't you?" she asked as she joined him in the kitchen.

"Yeah." He reached into the fridge and came out with mayonnaise, ketchup, and mustard. "Until my sister moved back to Dallas, the people at the station were the only family I had."

Lexi's heart ached at the reminder of what happened to Dane's parents all those years ago. She was glad he and his sister had reconnected. While her family might drive her crazy, she wouldn't trade them for anything.

"You mentioned the other night that you're a Texas girl, but I never did get a chance to ask you exactly where you're from," Dane said as they sat at the tiny table in the eat-in kitchen.

She blinked as he squirted a big dollop of mustard on his plate then dipped some fries in it. He must have seen her staring because he offered the mustard to her. "You want some?"

"No, thanks. I think I'll stick with ketchup." Lexi watched in amazement as he dunked another fry into the spicy stuff. "How can you eat that much mustard all at once? I might put a little bit on a sandwich, but no way would I even think of putting it on fries. In fact, I think Melinda and I have probably had the same bottle of mustard in our fridge for two years."

Which was kind of gross, now that she thought about it.

He dipped an onion ring into the same puddle of mustard and wolfed it down. "I don't know why, but I've always loved mustard on everything."

Lexi suddenly pictured Dane bringing mustard into the bedroom to slather on her. Okay...not going there.

"I'm from San Marcos," she said when she finally got around to answering his question. She took a few onion rings from where he'd dumped them on a plate and stacked them on her burger. "It's halfway between Austin and San Antonio. Kind of quiet compared to a city like Dallas, but it was a nice place to grow up."

"Does your family still live there?"

She nodded, grabbing another onion ring and crunching into it. "Two brothers and two sisters, along with a whole bushel load of cousins, nieces and nephews. I'm the only one who ever moved away from home for more than a couple years. Both sisters and one of my brothers went off to college, but they all moved back to San Marcos after graduation."

As they ate, Lexi found herself telling him about her family and all the crazy things she and her siblings did growing up. Like the time she and her sisters decided to have a picnic with their teddy bears when she, Heidi, and Misti were four, six, and eight respectively.

"The only problem was that there was a herd of free roaming cattle who thought the lush field of grass was the perfect place to graze," she said. "As you can imagine, the bull wasn't too happy with us. He chased us and our teddy bears right out of there."

Dane chuckled.

"Don't laugh! I was afraid of cows for years after that. Something which my brothers tease me about to this day." Lexi picked up her drink. "Which is when I remind them of the doofuses they made of themselves at the state fair."

"Okay, I'll bite," Dane said with a grin. "What'd they do?"

Lexi sipped her chocolate shake. "Drew volunteered to sit on the seat over the dunk tank. He wouldn't have minded getting dunked except Craig rigged the mechanism to dunk him every time someone threw a ball at the target regardless if they hit it or not. Drew was so pissed he chased Craig around the fairgrounds throwing baseballs at him."

Dane snorted out a laugh. "Sounds like

something Jax and I would have done in high school. And Skye would have never let us live it down either." Out of fries, he dipped his burger in mustard. "Your family seems really close."

"We are," she admitted. "I visit every year for Christmas and any other chance I can get. How about you and your sister? Do you two spend the holidays together?"

He finished chewing his burger before answering. "We haven't done that for a long time, but now that she's back in Dallas, I think we're going to start. I look forward to making up for all the time we lost when she was living in New York City."

"She sounds pretty awesome," Lexi said. "I can't wait to meet her."

"You up for stopping by to see her tomorrow at the ranch? I'll give her a call and make sure she'll be there."

"I'd love to! You sure she won't be too busy? She and Jax are getting married next week, right?"

Dane shook his head. "Nah. We'll hang out for a little while, maybe spend some time with the horses then get out of their way."

That sounded good to Lexi, especially the part about the horses. She'd ridden a lot when she was younger and never got tired of being around such beautiful animals.

"Do you want to go see a movie or something?" Dane asked after they finished eating.

She shook her head. "We don't have to

go anywhere if you don't want to. I'm fine with hanging around here."

"Want to catch something on Netflix then?" He flashed her a grin. "I'll even break out the popcorn."

She returned his smile. "As long as I get to pick what we watch. Or you'll have us watching some meaningless action flick."

He put on a hurt expression. "Meaningless? I'm insulted. All action flicks have meaning. Car chases, things blowing up—what more could you want?"

Lexi laughed. She could think of a few things, one of them being romance, but she didn't tell him that.

A few minutes later, the two of them were snuggled up on Dane's big couch with the lights turned down, a bowl of popcorn on the coffee table in front of them, and a horror movie about zombies chasing people around the mountains of Norway on the ginormous TV mounted on the living room wall. Lexi suspected Dane had gone for the scary movie thinking she'd end up snuggling close to him looking for protection from the evil zombies. Little did he know she didn't need an excuse to do that. But if it helped him think he was clever, she wouldn't ruin it for him.

It wasn't long before she lost interest in zombies—as hard as that was to believe. Then again, there was something a lot more stimulating than a silly horror flick to hold her attention. Dane must have thought so, too, because when she turned toward him, he gently cupped her face and pulled her in for a kiss.

Dane's mouth was hot on hers, his tongue insistent as it plunged in to find hers. She kissed him back as urgently, her tongue tangling with his. She'd never been with a guy who could take her breath away with a kiss.

"You taste good," he breathed, drawing her lower lip into his mouth and gently sucking on it.

Lexi could only moan in reply. Pulling away, she swung her leg over his, climbing on his lap. It blocked his view of the TV, but she didn't think he'd mind.

She smiled. "That's better."

Dane ran his hands up her bare thighs and leaned in close to nuzzle her neck. "I agree."

Lexi let out a sigh as the light trace of stubble along his jaw brushed against her skin. She grabbed a handful of his dark hair, silently urging him to continue even as he kissed his way up her neck. His big hands moved up her thighs, cupping her ass.

As Dane's mouth closed over hers again, Lexi couldn't miss the hard-on in his cargo shorts. The tingle she'd felt between her legs last night when they'd made out in her apartment was now an intense, throbbing need, and she rotated her hips to ease the ache there.

It occurred to her this was only their second date. Not that she'd ever had any kind of three-date rule when it came to sleeping with a guy. She always followed her instincts when it came to stuff like this. And, right now, those instincts were telling her Dane was special, and that she was more than ready to make love with him.

Dane must have been thinking the same thing because he slid his hands under the hem of her shirt. Lexi quivered at the feel of his fingers on her bare skin, holding her breath as he moved them higher.

His hands were inches from her breasts when a loud *ding-dong* echoed in her ears. She was vaguely aware it was the doorbell, but Dane ignored it, so she did, too. It rang again, only this time it was followed by a loud knock.

"Hey, Dane!" a man's voice called. "You in there?"

Dane dragged his mouth from hers with a muttered curse. "I better answer it before that idiot breaks down the damn door."

Lexi groaned, reluctantly climbing off him and onto the couch.

"I'll get rid of him," Dane said as he got up.

She wasn't sure who "that idiot" was, but when Dane opened the door, she realized it was Tory and another firefighter from Station 58, Kole Brandt. Neither of her coworkers seemed surprised to see her there. In fact, they both grinned broadly as they walked past Dane into the apartment without an invitation. She guessed that when Dane said the other guys at the station were like family, he really meant it.

Tory had two pizza boxes in one hand and a six-pack of beer in the other while Kole carried a video game and another six-pack.

"Since the new Call of Duty dropped today, we figured we'd come over and surprise you." Dark eyes dancing, Kole grinned as he tossed the game to Dane. "That way you can get in some practice before we play it at the station. You know, so you don't embarrass yourself?"

Dane scowled. "To be embarrassed, I'd have to play worse than you guys, and that's never going to happen."

Lexi couldn't help laughing. She might not be thrilled they got interrupted when things were getting interesting, but she couldn't hold it against Tory and Kole. The guys were here to mess with them. After seeing the way they ribbed each other at the station, she should have expected it.

Dane glanced at her, a resigned look on his face. "You ever play Call of Duty?"

"I have two brothers, remember? Of course I play." She grinned. "I'll even go first, so you three can see how it's supposed to be done."

Tory and Kole let out a whoop and high-fived.

"Sounds like an all-night gaming marathon to me," Tory said. "Let's get it started!"

Lexi would rather have an all-night sex

marathon with Dane—and the way he was looking at her, he would, too—but it wasn't like they could throw Tory and Kole out. Not without the guys knowing exactly what was going on and ribbing the hell out of them at the station for it.

Chapter Seven

I'M SO GLAD you guys came," Skye said with a smile as she hugged Lexi. "I was starting to think my brother was keeping you away from me on purpose."

"Now why would I do that?" Dane asked drily as he followed Lexi into the building.

He nodded at Jax then inhaled deeply through the nose. It smelled like more cake...and maybe something Italian. He wondered if his sister needed a neutral third party to taste anything.

Skye made a face as she came over and hugged him, too. "Maybe you're worried I'll tell her about all your bad habits, like that disgusting thing you do with French fries and mustard."

Lexi laughed. "Too late. I saw that last night. And as long as he doesn't try and convince me to put mustard on my fries, I'm fine with it."

Dane smirked at his sister. "See? Lexi

accepts me for who I am, mustard addiction and all."

Skye folded her arms. "Great. So I guess you've told her you sing in your sleep?"

"He does what?" Lexi asked in surprise.

"Oh yeah," Skye said. "He used to hum and sing theme songs from old TV shows in his sleep."

Dane flushed. "I haven't done that since I was a teenager."

Leave it to his sister to embarrass him. Hopefully, she wouldn't bring up any of the names of any of those shows because he used to watch some really lame stuff—as in old reruns from the sixties, seventies, and eighties. Think *Gilligan's Island*, *SWAT*, and even *Wonder Woman*. The first two he might be able to get away with, but Lexi would never let him live that last one down.

Fortunately, Skye didn't get into it. Instead, she gave Lexi a quick tour of the place and told her about the events she was currently catering.

"My sisters and I used to love making cupcakes with my mom when we were little," Lexi said with a smile. "We couldn't wait for them to cool off after they came out of the oven so we could frost them."

Skye's eyes lit up. "Jax and I were about to start frosting these when you guys came in. You want to help?"

Dane opened his mouth to remind his sister what happened the last time he'd helped her frost cupcakes, but Lexi was already nodding, clearly thrilled with the idea. A few minutes later, they were all standing around the granite topped island frosting several dozen cupcakes.

As it turned out, he ended up having a way better time than he thought he would. He quickly discovered that he loved doing anything with Lexi, even frosting cupcakes. They probably ate a lot more than they should have—and Skye had to redo quite a few of them—but it was fun hanging out together.

Dane watched transfixed as Lexi licked chocolate frosting off her finger. She must have caught him looking at her because she smiled. If his sister and future brother-in-law hadn't been there, he would have kissed her to see if the creamy confection tasted sweeter on her lips.

He stifled a groan. He'd never known a woman like Lexi. She could turn him on with a look, a smile—hell, even a snap of her fingers. And if Tory and Kole hadn't shown up last night and interrupted them, Dane was sure he and Lexi would have ended up in bed. Talk about the ultimate cockblock.

"Jax and I need to deliver these cupcakes," Skye said as they finished frosting them. "You guys want to hang around here and we can have dinner when we get back?"

Dane gave Lexi a questioning look. She smiled and nodded.

"Sounds good," he said. "I wanted to show Lexi the horses anyway."

As he and Lexi helped box the cupcakes, Dane mentioned to Skye he thought it was cool that she had little boxes with cutouts to hold up the cupcakes and her catering company's name—*Her Kitchen*—emblazoned across the lid.

Skye elbowed him in the ribs as she led the way outside to the delivery truck. "Hey. This is a serious business. I'm not messing around."

Dane only chuckled.

After Skye and Jax left, Dane led Lexi over to the barn and introduced her to the horses.

"This guy is called Big Joe," he said as they stopped in front of a stall occupied by a huge black stallion. "He's the player of the ranch, always trying to woo the ladies."

Lexi smiled as she ran her hand down Big Joe's strong neck. "That explains why he's making moon eyes at that girl."

Dane glanced over at the chestnut mare in the stall on the other side of the barn. "Probably. Then again, according to Jax, Star is immune to Big Joe's charm, so it could be a case of him fixating on the one horse who doesn't want him."

Lexi laughed. "I can't believe that. Big Joe is a very handsome horse. Aren't you, boy?"

Dane couldn't help grinning as Lexi moved from one stall to the other. She really loved horses. When they reached the stall holding a dappled-gray mare and her light-gray colt, Lexi actually squeed.

"He's so cute!" she said, immediately leaning over one of the side rails to gently glide her hand over the colt's withers.

Momma mare eyed Lexi suspiciously but must have figured she wasn't a danger to her offspring because she went back to her oats.

Dane rested his forearms on the edge of the stall door. He'd seen the colt a few times now and noticed that his coat was getting a little darker with each visit. The horse would probably be the same color as his mother soon. "This little fella is Smoke."

Lexi smiled. "Appropriate name since he's gray."

"True, but Jax and Skye named him Smoke because he was born right after the barn that used to stand on this same spot was burned to the ground by some psychopath who was obsessed with Skye. In fact, Jax and I could still smell the smoke in the air as we helped his mom, Lulu, give birth to him."

Lexi's eyes widened. "Don't think you're going to get away with saying something like that and not telling me the rest of the story. What the heck happened?"

Dane chuckled. "Okay. Why don't we take Lulu and Smoke for a walk while we talk?"

Lexi glanced down at her sleeveless dress and low-heeled shoes. "Sandals out in the pasture?"

"Sure. Pay attention to where you're

stepping and you'll be fine."

He got a halter and lead lines on the two horses then let Lexi take Smoke as they headed for the main pasture. As they walked, he told her about the man who'd tried to kill Skye—and him—by burning the old barn down around them.

"He was a friend from New York? What kind of man does something that crazy?" Lexi slanted him a look. "How badly were you hurt?"

"Not too bad," he said, trying to downplay how much danger he'd been in during the whole situation. "The guy knocked me out, that's all."

Lexi frowned. "That's all?"

He grinned. "I have a hard head." When she gave him a skeptical look, he added, "It was one of those weird once-in-a-lifetime type of things. It's a safe bet to say that nothing like that is ever going to happen again."

Lexi didn't look too sure about that, so Dane steered the conversation in another direction.

"Since you love horses I'm surprised you don't have one."

She shrugged. "I'd love a horse, but I don't have anywhere to keep one."

"I'm sure Jax and Skye would be willing to let you stable him—or her—here."

Lexi considered that. "You really think so?"

"Sure," Dane smiled. "They board horses

all the time."

"Huh." She ran her free hand affectionately down Smoke's neck. "You know, I might think about that."

Dane and Lexi were brushing the two horses down a little while later when Jax walked into the barn.

"I think I'm in love with Smoke." Lexi smiled at Jax. "If he'd fit in my apartment, I'd take him home with me tonight."

Jax chuckled. "I think Lulu might have something to say about that. But maybe if you can fit both of them in your place?"

She made a face. "Probably not."

"Well, you can visit Smoke as much as you want then," Jax said. "Skye wanted to know if you wanted to help pick something out for dinner. Dane will eat anything she makes, but she thought you might have a few special requests."

Lexi shook her head. "Not really, but I'll go in anyway." She patted Smoke on the neck and said she'd see him later then gave Dane a kiss. "Have fun."

"You and Lexi look good together," Jax said after she left. He picked up a brush and ran it over Smoke's flanks. "I don't think I've ever seen you look so comfortable with a woman before."

Dane grinned. "Yeah, I know. I'm not sure what it is about Lexi, but we click."

Jax lifted a brow. "You sure that's not because you two are sleeping together?"

"I doubt it since we haven't gone there

yet."

On the other side of Smoke, Jax did a double take. "Seriously? I thought for sure you had. Well, if anyone deserves to have someone special in their life, it's you. Skye's going to be thrilled."

Dane slanted him a hard look. "Don't you dare tell her I said any of that. The next thing you know she'll be asking Lexi what flavor cake she wants at our wedding."

It wasn't that he didn't want to get married someday, but he and Lexi had only gone on a few dates. *Sheesh.*

Jax chuckled. "I won't mention it to Skye. I don't think that's going to matter, though. If I picked up on the vibe between you and Lexi, she will, too.

"Wonderful," Dane muttered.

"Come on." Jax clapped him in the shoulder. "Let's get Lulu and Smoke back in their stalls then go inside before Skye starts digging all this stuff out of Lexi on her own."

* * * * *

Lexi stopped outside the door of the house to check her shoes and made sure she wasn't tracking anything in. She'd loved taking Lulu and Smoke for a walk, but when she came back to do it again, she'd remember to wear jeans and boots. A sleeveless dress and flip-flops weren't the right outfit for this kind of stuff.

She smiled to herself as she thought

about how Jax had gotten her and Dane separated. It'd been obvious he wanted to talk to Dane alone, most likely about her. That was okay since she wanted to talk to Skye, too, and get the scoop on her big brother.

Lexi knocked then opened the door and stuck her head in. "Skye? Jax said you needed some help with dinner."

"Come on in," Skye called. "I'm in the kitchen."

Lexi stepped inside and closed the door then turned to see a black lab standing in the entryway regarding her with a curious expression on his furry face.

"Um...hello there," she said.

He looked friendly, but she wasn't sure if she should pet the guy or be concerned that he might not let her pass.

"That's Rodeo," Skye said. "Scratch his ears and he'll love you forever."

She took Skye's advice, crouching down to ruffle the lab's big ears. It worked like a charm. Rodeo gave her a doggy smile, his eyes all drowsy and happy.

Giving his head another pat, Lexi stood and walked through the living room with its stone fireplace, big sectional couch, and ginormous flat-screen TV into the adjoining kitchen where Skye was rolling out biscuits.

Lexi inhaled appreciatively. "Something smells delicious."

"Thanks. It's beef stew." Skye jerked her head at the slow cooker on the granite countertop. "Can you give it a stir?"

Lexi washed and dried her hands then used the big spoon Skye had set out to stir the savory stew.

"Dane told me about how you and Jax got together," Lexi said. "Something about a guy following you all the way from New York City to kill you and Jax saving your life? That's crazy—and romantic as hell, I have to admit."

Skye laughed as she cut out perfectly round biscuits and placed them on a cookie sheet. "It didn't feel so romantic while it was happening, but afterward I realized I wouldn't change a minute of it. Okay...that's not quite true. There are quite a few things I definitely would have changed. The parts where Jax and Dane almost got killed certainly come to mind. But ultimately, I'm very happy with how it all turned out."

"I don't blame you." Lexi put the lid back on the slow cooker with a smile. "Between finding a guy as hunky as Jax and the way your business is starting off, things seem to be going really well for you."

"They are," Skye agreed as she slipped the cookie sheet into the oven and closed the door. "But that's not the best part. The thing I'm most grateful for is the fact that I've found a man who believes in me and supports me. He's never suggested that what I'm attempting is crazy or too big for me. Instead, he finds a way to help me get to where I want to be. I never knew how important that quality was in a man until I found it with Jax." She opened the cabinet over the dishwasher and took out four dinner bowls and four small plates. "What about you and Dane?"

Lexi was tempted to fib, afraid Skye might not like the idea of her and Dane moving too fast, but then realized that was silly.

"I know we just started going out, but I have to admit, I'm already falling for him," she said. It was true. A couple of dates and she was already thinking long-term with him. "Do you think that's crazy?"

"Not at all." Skye's lips curved. "Who we fall for—or how fast—doesn't have to follow any rules. It simply happens. The smart people are the ones who recognize that and let it happen. The crazy ones are the idiots who overthink everything and screw it up." She moved around the table in the kitchen, setting down the bowls and plates. "I had a crush on Jax when I was younger and knew he was the one for me the minute I came back to Dallas. I didn't care how long we'd been seeing each other."

Lexi leaned back against the granite island with a grin. "Now I don't feel so bad admitting I transferred to Station 58 so I could meet Dane."

Skye looked at her in surprise. "You did?"

"Uh-huh. I ran into Dane at an incident scene a couple months ago and couldn't get those dreamy dark eyes of his out of my head."

"I knew there was a reason I liked you the moment we met," Skye said. "You're a woman after my own heart. You saw what you wanted and you went after it."

Lexi watched Skye collect cutlery from the drawer. "Do you think Dane and I have what it takes to make a relationship work?"

Skye's expression was thoughtful as she placed a spoon and knife beside each bowl. "Yeah, I do. I mean, it's hard for firefighters and paramedics to find people who understand what they do for a living and the crazy hours they work. Believe me, I know. Not only do you and Dane already work the same shift at the station, but you have the whole living-the-life-of-danger thing down pat. That's got to count in your favor, right? Besides, if I know my brother—and I do—he's already head over heels for you."

Lexi hoped she was right.

"Speaking of which, has my brother gotten around to asking you to the wedding yet?" Skye continued.

Lexi shook her head. "I think he's probably worried it might send the wrong message since we've only gone out a few times. You know how guys can be about weddings."

Skye scowled. "That's stupid—and so typical. I'll ask you then. Would you like to come? Jax and I would love to have you there."

"I'd love to."

Lexi hoped it wouldn't be weird for Dane. Yeah, they were dating, but some guys could be funny about stuff like that.

Skye looked like she wanted to say more, but Dane and Jax walked in the back door. Dane gave Rodeo an affectionate pet then straightened with a grin.

"Smells great," he said.

Skye glanced over her shoulder as she opened the oven. "Wash up. Dinner's almost ready."

Dane chuckled. "Yes, ma'am."

While Dane waited for Jax to finish at the sink, Lexi slipped up beside him and mentioned Skye had invited her to the wedding.

"You don't mind that I said yes, do you?" she added.

He smiled. "Of course not. I wanted to invite you myself, but I didn't want to put you in the awkward position of saying no if weddings weren't your thing."

Lexi almost laughed when she realized she'd been worried about putting him on the spot. But Dane didn't seem freaked out by the idea at all. "I think it will be fun."

He leaned in to kiss her. "Me, too."

During dinner, the conversation quickly turned to shop talk. Skye didn't seem to mind, but Lexi noticed Jax steered clear of any of the more dangerous calls he'd gone on. He mentioned he'd talked to Captain Stewart earlier, though. According to their boss, there'd been several more car crashes around Dallas thanks to those crazy street racers. Clearly, those jackasses didn't care if anyone got hurt.

As Skye smoothly changed the subject to talk about the upcoming wedding and where they were going on their honeymoon, Lexi felt Dane's sock-covered foot caress the inside of her calf. She looked up to see him sitting across from her looking like butter wouldn't melt in his mouth. His foot moved a little higher until he was teasing the inside of her thigh. She slipped off her flip-flop and responded in kind, tracing her bare toes along his jean-clad calf then up his leg.

They took turns playing footsie with each other under the table for the remainder of the meal, all the while trying not to give anything away. Messing around while Skye and Jax were none the wiser was fun—and hot. Lexi even slipped her toes all the way up to Dane's crotch to caress the bulge there. On the other side of the table, Dane sucked in a breath. She hid her smile in her glass of iced tea. That had definitely gotten his attention. Speaking of things at attention, he had a heck of a hard-on hidden in those jeans.

When Skye and Jax got up to clear the table after dinner, Dane sat there for an extra five minutes, no doubt worried the bulge in his jeans might give them away. By the time Skye brought over dessert—chocolate cupcakes filled with coffee mousse and topped with chocolate frosting—he seemed to be back in control. Lexi was tempted to start up another game of footsie under the table, but behaved herself.

"I had fun today," Dane said to her a few hours later as they pulled out of Jax and Skye's driveway onto the road and headed back to the city.

"Me, too." Lexi grinned as she snuggled closer to him. "Especially playing footsie with you under the table. I haven't done anything like that since I was a teenager. Hope you don't mind my teasing you like that."

Dane chuckled. "I definitely didn't mind. But I do intend to get you back for it later."

Lexi quivered at the promise in those words. Even though they both had to be up early to get to the station for their shift, she didn't want the evening to end.

She rested her hand on his thigh and leaned in a little more. "What do you think about going back to your place for a while so we can pick up where we left off?"

He stopped at the corner and turned his head to look at her. The light from the streetlamp glinted off his dark eyes, making her breath hitch. "You sure about that?"

She nodded, not trusting herself to speak.

"That works for me," he said.

Mouth curving into a sexy smile, he turned right instead of left and headed toward his place.

Chapter Eight

DANE COULDN'T REALLY blame Lexi for teasing him during dinner since he'd started the game of erotic footsie under the table with her in the first place. And while his hard-on had eased up a little bit while they had dessert, it had come back in full force on the drive to his apartment. When she'd put her hand on his thigh, he'd been ready to put the truck in park and pull her onto his lap right there.

Pulling into his parking space, he cut the engine and opened his door then climbed out and offered his hand to Lexi. She took it without a word and, together, they practically ran up the stairs to his apartment.

The moment they walked inside, Lexie spun around and kissed him hard. Dane urged her back against the door, holding her there with his body as he explored her mouth. She got a hand between them, sliding it down his abs to caress his erection.

Damn. It felt like his cock was going to burst through his jeans.

He kept his hands pressed against the door over her head as their tongues tangled with each other. Keeping his mitts off her steaming hot body was the only way to make sure he didn't rip off her dress and take her right there.

But the hand caressing his hard-on proved to be his undoing, and he finally weaved his fingers into her long hair, yanking her head back and kissing her fiercely, taking her mouth like he wanted.

Lexi moaned, spreading her legs a little to grind against his thigh through her dress at the same time she gave his shaft a firm squeeze. He was so caught up in how good it felt, he barely realized his other hand had wandered down to cup her bottom. She had absolutely the finest ass he'd ever had the privilege of touching. It was firm but curvy, and oh-so-squeezable.

She clutched his shoulder with one hand, sighing against his mouth.

"You like when I do that?" he asked.

"Mmm," she breathed.

He bunched the material of her dress in his hand, pulling it up until he was grabbing one panty-covered cheek. The sound of pleasure Lexi let out almost made him want to tear off her barely-there panties. Telling his inner caveman to chill, he dragged his mouth away and rested his forehead against hers.

"I'm not sure I can hold out long enough to make it to the bedroom," he rasped.

She let out a husky laugh. "Who says our first time has to be in a bed?"

Dane groaned.

Catching the hem of her dress, he slowly lifted it over her head and tossed it in the general direction of the couch. Lexi kicked off her sandals and unsnapped her lacy bra even as he yanked his shirt off and sent it searching for her dress. Instead of stripping off his jeans, he stopped and stared.

Lexi stood there wearing nothing but a skimpy pair of panties. He'd seen her in the bikini earlier, so he'd already known she was in fantastic shape, but seeing her perfectly rounded breasts with their subtle tan lines and dusky-pink nipples made him realize how amazing she truly was. He could stand there the rest of the night and simply gaze at her.

She slipped her fingers in the waistband of her panties and slowly shoved them down over her hips with the sexiest damn wiggle he'd ever seen. When the scrap of material pooled on the floor between her legs, she gracefully stepped out of them and walked toward him.

Giving him a sultry smile, she reached for his belt.

Dane captured her small hands in his much larger ones before she could unbuckle it, tugging her forward against his bare chest as he pulled her wrists behind her back and held them there. Lexi didn't seem to mind being his prisoner, but he didn't give her a chance to say anything as he covered her mouth with his and slipped his tongue inside to tease and play.

She moaned as he glided his free hand over her body, paying specific attention to her breasts and her nipples. Then he moved lower, running his hand down the center of her taut abs past her belly button and through the collection of curls at the junction of her thighs before finally delving into the folds of her pussy to tease her clit.

Lexi whimpered as he slipped his finger inside her wetness. Then he very slowly began to move in and out as he pressed the palm of his hand to the sensitive area at the top of her cleft. She trembled, and if he hadn't been holding onto her wrists, she probably would have collapsed to the floor.

She writhed against his hand, moaning. It would have been so incredibly easy to make her come that way. But while he wanted her to climax, there was a very special way he wanted to make it happen.

He slipped his hand out from between her legs, ignoring her complaints as he took her hand and led her into the living room. Spinning her around, he nudged her until she was sitting on the back of the couch, her toes off the floor and confusion clear on her face.

Grinning, he grabbed her thighs, lifting them up and spreading them wide as he moved between her legs.

Eyes widening, Lexi clutched at his arms

with a breathy giggle. "Are you crazy? I'm going to fall off."

Dane leaned over and slowly kissed his way down her inner thigh. "You're not going to fall. You're going to come...until you scream."

He didn't tease her, not even a little. He'd already done that with his fingers, and she was clearly ready for more. So after he ran his tongue carefully up and down the folds of her pussy a few times, he settled his mouth over her clit and began to gently lick there.

Lexi's whole body went rigid. Dane tightened his hold on her thighs, keeping her in place as he lazily moved his tongue back and forth over the most sensitive part of her body. Her taste was intoxicating, making him hungry for more of her while making him hard as hell at the same time.

She did indeed scream when she orgasmed, dropping her head back and biting down on her knuckles in an attempt to muffle the sound. It didn't work, of course. The echoes of her pleasure bounced off every wall in his apartment.

Dane had never been with a woman who gave in to her pleasure like Lexi did. Watching her body writhe as he continued to lap at her clit was the most beautiful thing he'd ever seen.

He held onto her until she got herself back under control, not letting go until she raised her head and looked at him. The heat in her blue eyes made him groan. Licking her lips, Lexi languidly slid off the back of the couch and onto her knees in front of him.

"My turn," she said, a wicked smile crossing her face as she popped open the buttons on his 501s.

* * * * *

After the hard orgasm Dane had given her, it took Lexi longer than she would have liked to get his jeans off. But once she had them yanked down to mid-thigh, it got easier. After that, his underwear was a piece of cake, even though she had to work carefully to free the serious bulge hidden in there. When he was completely naked, she sat back on her heels and appreciated what a hunk he was.

Damn, what a body. Abs so cut she could wash her clothes on them, pecs and shoulders muscled enough to give her a visual orgasm, powerfully strong thighs, and a cock so thick and perfect, she wasn't sure if she should cry or cheer. She decided to go for option number three and simply worship it.

Reaching out, she wrapped her hand around the base of the shaft and tugged him close, taking him into her mouth the second he was within range.

Dane groaned as her lips closed over the head. She closed her eyes, echoing the sentiment with a moan of her own. She couldn't help it. He tasted so unbelievable good.

She fluttered her tongue over the tip then took him completely into her mouth, moving her head in time with her hands, working him slow and sensually. She was going to make him come exactly like he'd done to her.

Lexi was getting a good rhythm going when Dane reached down and dragged her to her feet.

"Hey, I was working down there," she pointed out.

He ignored her, scooping her off her feet and carrying her into the bedroom. *He was really strong*. Which wasn't an excuse for interrupting her blow job, but it was definitely a valid observation.

Dane tossed her into the middle of his big bed then dug a condom out of his nightstand and joined her. She helped him roll the condom down, refusing to be a passive participant in any part of this evening. Then she lay back with a smile and spread her legs wide as he climbed between them.

He planted his big, strong arms on either side of her shoulders then leaned down until his face was mere inches from hers. Pulse quickening, she found it impossible to look anywhere but into those warm chocolate-brown eyes of his.

"Do you have any idea how incredibly sexy you are?" he whispered as he closed the distance between them and kissed her softly.

She hoped that was a rhetorical question, because she wouldn't know how to answer it even if she could have spoken. Instead, she focused on returning Dane's kiss and pulling him down on top of her. Dane held back only long enough to get himself positioned right so that when Lexi wrapped her legs around his waist and urged him close, his perfect shaft slid in like they were made for each other.

Lexi gasped as he filled her. Grabbing a handful of his hair, she kissed him harder. When Dane started to move, it felt so good she nearly cried. His thrusts started slow and smooth, but built quickly to a wild pounding that sent spirals of pleasure through her. The sensations were so overwhelming, she buried her face in the curve of his neck and shoulder and urged him on, locking her heels together behind his back and yanking him in harder with each thrust.

When her climax hit, she buried her face deeper in his shoulder and screamed as a lightning-fast orgasm zipped through her like a runaway train. She squeezed her legs tightly around him when her pleasure crested then kept going on and on and on.

She wasn't sure when it happened, but at some point, Dane flipped them both over until she was riding on top of him. This position drove his cock even deeper, triggering another surge of sensations that left her crying out.

She both felt and heard it when Dane came. He grabbed her hips and slammed himself into her as far as he could go, letting out a hoarse groan as he poured himself into her.

Afterward, Lexi collapsed forward onto Dane's strong chest like a limp ragdoll as the last of the tremors dissipated, leaving her weak as a kitten. She lay there with her face against his chest, gasping for breath. That had to be the best sex of her life.

"That was amazing," she whispered.

He ran a hand over her hair. "Ditto."

Lexi wasn't sure how long they lay there like that, but at some point she finally found the energy to look at the clock and realized it was after midnight. They had to be at the station at seven. Crap, they were both going to be so tired tomorrow at work.

She pushed herself up off Dane's warm, inviting chest. "It's getting late."

He twirled her hair around his finger. "I'll drive you home, if that's what you want. But, if you're asking, I'd rather you stay the night."

Lexi blinked. Not in surprise, but because she was taken aback by the depth of emotion she saw in his eyes. She might have had the greatest orgasm of all time, but her heart was beating even faster now.

"Are you sure you don't mind getting up early to drive me back to my place so I can change and grab some stuff?" she asked.

She wasn't asking because she needed

him to talk her into staying. Falling asleep in his arms was the perfect way to end the perfect day.

Dane pulled her against him and kissed her long and slow. "Hell no, I don't mind." His mouth curved. "Although I don't know about waking up early since I don't plan on letting you get any sleep tonight anyway."

Lexi laughed as Dane rolled her onto her back and trailed kisses along her body. If he was thinking about round two, she was definitely down with that.

Chapter Nine

LATE NIGHT?" TRENT asked, glancing at Lexi as he pulled their rescue truck out of the hospital parking lot and headed for the highway on-ramp.

She'd tried to hide her yawn behind her hand, but Trent must have seen it anyway. While she was tired partly thanks to making love with Dane half the night, the constant string of calls she and Trent had gone on today probably had something to do with it, too. It had been one long day of nonstop car wrecks, chest pains, trips, slips, falls, industrial mishaps, and poor athletic decisions.

"Yeah," she said in answer to Trent's question. "Dane and I went over to Jax's ranch yesterday and didn't get home until almost midnight."

Trent checked his side mirrors as he merged onto I-635. Traffic was still crazy even at eight o'clock at night. Around them, drivers jockeyed for lane position as they approached the insanely confusing High Five Interchange that connected 635 to I-75 as well as several other surface roads. Five stacked levels of bridges, underpasses, and overpasses could get a bit tricky, and the rain didn't help.

"Sounds like things are working out well with you and Dane," he said as he switched on his indicator and changed lanes.

Lexi smiled. "They are."

Actually, saying things were going well with Dane was an understatement. Things were going awesome. Then again, maybe she was a little biased considering Dane had completely worn her out last night. The guy was absolutely amazing in bed. And on the floor, too, now that she thought about it. She'd never had a night like it. Hell, if you combined the last three or four times she'd slept with a man, they still wouldn't add up to what she'd experienced with Dane last night.

"What about you?" she asked Trent. "Was Tish in town?"

Tish was a flight attendant Trent had met a while back. She was based out of DFW but was gone a lot more than she was home, so getting together was difficult, especially with Trent's work schedule.

He shook his head. "Nah. She texted me on Sunday saying she got transferred to LAX. Neither of us was interested in making the long distance thing work."

Lexi frowned. "Dang. I'm sorry. I know

you were starting to get serious about her."

Trent shrugged as he took the overpass. "Don't be. I get the feeling Tish requested the transfer so she wouldn't have to actually break up with me."

"Well, that sucks," Lexi said.

She was wondering if she should mention Melinda was interested in him when Trent jerked the wheel to the side, almost sliding the rescue truck right off the overpass.

"What the...?"

Lexi's words trailed off as three cars zipped around them, one of them nearly spinning out of control as the driver clipped the front left bumper of the rescue truck.

"Shit!" Trent swore as he fought for control of the wheel on the wet, slippery pavement.

Lexi grabbed the dash, muttering a curse as the three cars darted in and around the traffic ahead of them. It was those damn street racers. Apparently, they didn't give a crap that there was no place for the other drivers to go on the overpass as they jammed themselves through the congestion.

Trent had gotten their vehicle going straight again when one of the racers tried to force his way between two cars, sideswiping a small sedan driving in the right lane. The impact sent the sedan sliding out of control on the wet pavement and spinning in a slow circle. All Lexi could do was watch as the sedan slammed into the concrete and metal railing on the side of the overpass and kept right on going.

Lexi's breath caught in her throat. If the car went over the retaining wall, it would be a hundred and twenty foot drop to the traffic on I-75. Even if the people in the car made it through the fall, they wouldn't survive getting rammed by the traffic flying along the road beneath them. But somehow the car stopped, partially wedged in the debris of the broken wall.

Trent floored the engine, trying to get to the car as fast as he could even as the back of the sedan tilted up and down as the rear wheels came off the road.

The street racers were long gone by the time she and Trent reached the sedan, but Lexi no longer cared about them. She was focused entirely on the small car teetering on the brink of the overpass railing. It looked like the thing was going to go over any second.

Trent slammed to a stop less than ten feet from the car, sliding sideways to block the rightmost lane of traffic and hitting the switch for the flashing lights.

"I'll call this in then get a tow strap and try to keep the car from going any farther while you check on the people inside it," he said.

Lexi didn't even slow down to grab her gear but simply shoved open the door and ran for the car in the pounding rain. In the distance, she could hear police sirens as well as the distinct tones of a fire engine.

There was only one person in the car—a middle-aged woman with platinum blond hair and cuts all over her face.

"It's okay," Lexi told the woman through the open window on the driver's side. "My name is Lexi and I'm a paramedic. My partner and I are going to get you out of here. Don't move, okay?"

The woman turned tearful, terrified eyes on her. She nodded. "Hurry, please. I'm scared."

"We will," Lexi promised.

Lexi did a quick assessment of the car. The front of the vehicle was badly smashed up, and the steering column and part of the engine were shoved into the woman's lap. That would make getting her out quickly a problem.

Lexi's first instinct was to open the driver's door but she stopped herself. With the vehicle hanging over the edge of the wall, it was too dangerous. She surveyed the vehicle, checking for a better entrance while at the same time assessing how easy it would be to get the woman out another way. The back door on the driver's side was too crushed to function, and the front door on the passenger side was nearly as far out over empty space as the driver side door. If all that wasn't bad enough, the rear door on the passenger side was wedged against what remained of the concrete railing. It wasn't going to be easy to open.

That left only the sunroof.

The woman in the car turned her head slightly to look at Lexi, tears streaming down her face to mix with the raindrops. "You said you'd hurry!"

"We will," Lexi assured her gently. "Sit still, okay?"

The woman shoved open her door as if Lexi hadn't spoken. The steering wheel and remains of the airbag weren't going to let her go anywhere, however, something she quickly figured out. Panic filled her eyes, and she immediately began to struggle.

The front of the car tipped downward, sliding a little farther over the edge. That only freaked the poor woman out even more.

The vehicle was going over for sure. *Crap*.

"Don't move!" Lexi ordered over the woman's screams, putting a hand on her arm. "I'm going to help you, but you have to do as I say."

Lexi didn't wait for a reply, but instead raced to the back of the car and climbed up on the trunk, praying her weight would be enough to push the car back down.

It wasn't. The back of the car kept going up anyway.

Where the hell was Trent with that tow strap?

Out of nowhere, a big, burly white guy in a John Deere cap jumped on the back of the car beside her, quickly followed by a skinny black teenaged boy who probably weighed less than Lexi. She almost cried as their combined weight shoved the back of the car onto the road.

Then Trent was there with the big, heavy yellow tow strap, diving under the vehicle to wrap the strong material around the rear axle. He was out in a flash, racing back to the rescue truck and jumping behind the wheel. Shoving the ambulance in reverse, he started backing up.

The slack disappeared out of the two strap and from her position on the trunk, Lexi felt the back of the sedan twist down and away from the edge of the wall and the railing it was balanced on.

Suddenly, the woman screamed in pain. Lexi looked through the rain-spattered back window to see one of the woman's legs being crushed by a piece of metal sticking up from the floorboard of the car. Crap. It was a piece of rebar from the overpass retaining wall.

"Stop!" Lexi shouted over her shoulder, holding up a closed fist in Trent's direction.

He immediately hit the brake and leaned out the window of the truck. "What's wrong?"

"A piece of rebar from the concrete railing has punctured the bottom of the car and is pressing against the woman's leg," Lexi said, her wet ponytail swinging around to smack her in the back as she turned to look at him. "If you keep pulling, it's going to crush her."

"Shit!" he muttered.

Lexi carefully climbed off the trunk of the

car along with her two volunteers. At least the recovery strap would keep the car from going over—for now.

Trent got out of the truck and ran over to them. "I didn't get the vehicle far enough back to keep it stable. If it starts to tip forward again, I don't think the strap is going to hold it. We have to get her out of there."

He was right. *Dammit.*

"We're not getting her out through any of the doors," Lexi said. "I'll climb in through the sunroof and get her out that way."

All three men looked at her like she was insane.

"I'll go," Trent said.

Lexi shook her head. "I'm lighter than you are. Your weight would push the car over the edge."

Trent cursed. He opened his mouth to argue, but then closed it again. "You're right. Hang on while I grab some rope."

As Lexi waited for him to get it from the truck, she caught sight of the bystanders watching with a mix of trepidation and concern on their faces. She knew how they felt. But if she didn't get that poor woman out of there, she was going to die. And Lexi would be damned if she was going to let that happen.

"Tie this around your waist," Trent said, handing her the rope. "And be careful, okay?"

She nodded. "I will."

Lexi gave the knot she'd tied in the rope a tug. If the car went over, the rope might save her. Then again, if it caught on the vehicle as it fell, it could also kill her.

Taking a deep breath, she cautiously climbed onto the slippery trunk of the wet car and over the top until she reached the sunroof. The woman craned her neck to look up at her.

"What are you doing?" she demanded, her voice trembling.

"I'm going to get you out of there, like I promised," Lexi said, hoping her voice wasn't shaking as much as the rest of her. "Close your eyes, duck down, and put your hands over your head to protect yourself. I'm going to break the glass in the sunroof."

Taking the small glass breaking tool she always carried on her belt, she put the tip of it on the sunroof and pushed, shattering it into a million tiny pieces. Hooking the tool on her belt, she slithered through the roof and into the front seat of the car, avoiding the piece of rebar sticking up through the floorboard. The moment she did, the car started to slide forward again.

"Lexi, we have trouble out here," Trent shouted. "The car's weight is dragging the rescue truck across the wet pavement. You need to work fast."

The woman's eyes went wide, her tears coming faster. "Please don't let me die in here."

"I won't," Lexi said. "I promise."

She took the small tool off her belt again. In addition to breaking glass, it also cut through seatbelts. As she worked, she asked the woman her name.

"Debra Wallace."

Lexi smiled. "Another minute and I'm going to have you out of here, Debra."

Or she would have if the seatbelt had been the only thing standing between her and getting Debra to safety. Unfortunately, the steering wheel was wedged against Debra's legs, pinning her to the seat.

"Hang on, okay?"

Debra nodded.

Lexi reached under the seat for the latch to adjust it. Putting one foot against the dash and her shoulder against the driver's seat, she shoved at the same time she lifted the latch. It moved a few inches, but not quite enough.

Crap.

Releasing the latch, she turned around so that she was sitting on the console facing the front of the car. Then she put both feet on the steering wheel, shoving and kicking with everything she had. It moved, but so did the car.

"Lexi!" Trent shouted. "Hurry the hell up in there. We're losing the car!"

Lexi didn't waste time with a reply. She simply slid her arms under Debra's and dragged her out of the seat. Debra cried out in pain but shoved against the floorboard with her good leg, fighting to get herself out of there.

Since she couldn't get both Debra and

herself out at the same time, Lexi climbed through the sunroof first then reached in to grab the woman's arms. The car creaked, tipping forward again.

Tightening her hold on Debra, Lexi scampered backward, hauling her through the sunroof. It wasn't until Lexi reached the back of the car that she saw at least a dozen civilians doing everything they could from dragging on her safety rope, to holding onto the bumper of the sedan, to shoving against the front of the rescue truck at the same time to keep the car from going over the edge. But even with all of that and Trent putting the rescue truck in reverse, the weight of the car was too much for all of it. The sedan was going over, and there wasn't anything anyone could do to stop it.

Gritting her teeth, Lexi dragged the woman off the trunk, slamming onto the hard concrete of the road as the vehicle toppled. Lexi had enough time to realize she hadn't saved anyone yet. The car was taking the rescue truck and group of civilians with it.

Lexi shoved Debra to the side and jumped to her feet, praying the woman wouldn't get run over by the sliding rescue vehicle, when a loud voice broke through the insanity around her.

"Move!" a deep voice ordered.

A split second later, a huge fire axe came down and sliced through the towing strap in a single sweep of its razor sharp blade.

Lexi jerked her head up to see Dane standing there with axe in hand as the car fell from the overpass to the freeway below. She cringed, expecting to hear the horrific sound of other vehicles smashing into it, but all she heard was her pounding heart and the sound of the rain hitting the pavement. The police must have been able to clear the roadway in time. Thank God.

Only then did she wonder how the hell Dane had gotten up there since the whole overpass was jammed and jellied up with stopped traffic. He must have run all the way from the base of the overpass in full turnout gear.

She opened her mouth to ask him, but the words were drowned out as cheers went up in the crowd of onlookers around them. As the rain pelted her face, Lexi smiled up at Dane, having a crazy urge to drag him down for a kiss.

But that was going to have to wait until later. She still had to treat Debra's injuries and get her to the hospital.

Besides, Dane seemed a little too dazed at the moment for a kiss.

Chapter Ten

FORTUNATELY, BESIDES A broken left leg and a multitude of cuts and bruises, Debra Wallace was going to be fine. Though she had some pain in the chest, a look at her electrocardiogram told Lexi she didn't have any heart issues. The pain was almost certainly due to taking an airbag and a crushed steering wheel to the chest. Debra thanked Lexi so many times for saving her, she started to get embarrassed.

Right after that, the police showed up to talk to Lexi and Trent so another rescue truck transported Debra to the hospital. Lexi expected uniformed officers to take their statements and was surprised when a detective named Logan Maxwell introduced himself. Tall with dark hair and brown eyes, he was interested in anything they could tell him about the street racers.

"Honestly, I didn't get a good look at them," Lexi admitted. "All I saw was a flash of color speed by us."

Detective Maxwell looked at Trent. "What about you?"

Trent thought a moment. "I think one was a Mustang and I'm pretty sure I saw a tricked out Nissan. I didn't get any license plates, though."

The detective nodded. "Okay, thanks." He handed her and Trent his business card. "If you think of anything else, give me a call."

After Detective Maxwell left, Lexi looked around for Dane to see if he was still there, but he was nowhere in sight.

"You ready to head back to the station?" Trent asked.

She nodded. Besides wanting to see Dane, she needed to change into dry clothes. Even though the rain had stopped, they were still soaked.

After sitting in those wet clothes all the way back to the station, Lexi immediately headed upstairs to the women's locker room to change before she went in search of Dane. She'd reached the locker room when she heard footsteps behind her. She turned to see Dane striding toward her.

She opened her mouth to thank him for getting to that overpass at exactly the right time, but then she caught the look on his face and realized something was off. If she didn't know better, she'd think he was angry.

"What the hell did you think you were doing out there?" he demanded.

"What are you talking about?"

Dane scowled. "You know exactly what I'm talking about. That insane stunt you pulled on the overpass. Were you trying to get yourself killed?"

She blinked. Crap. He *was* angry. And now, so was she. "What kind of question is that? I was trying to save a woman's life. You, more than anyone, should recognize that."

"I never would have done anything that reckless," he snapped.

Lexi felt like he'd slapped her. Telling her she was reckless was the same as saying she wasn't good at her job. "It might have been risky, but it wasn't reckless, and it was the only choice we had. That car was about to go over the edge. What was I supposed to do? Let her die?"

"What you should have done was let Trent get her out."

She gaped at Dane. Thinking he'd been questioning her skill at her job had been bad enough. Questioning how she did that job because she was a woman instead of a man was even worse.

Lexi folded her arms and glared at him. "I see. So Trent gets to risk his life to save people because he's a man, but I can't because I'm a woman?"

"That's not what I said," he insisted.

"Really?" she countered. "Then what is going on here? You run into burning buildings nearly every day to save people, and I never call you on it. Yet, the first time you see me do something dangerous to save someone's life, you say I'm reckless. Tell me how I'm supposed to take that?"

Dane opened his mouth to say something—heaven help her, if it was one more stupid thing, she was not going to be responsible for what happened—but a deep voice interrupted him.

"What the hell is going on up here?"

Lexi and Dane both turned to see Captain Stewart standing there regarding them with a scowl on his face.

"Nothing, Captain," Dane said. "Lexi and I disagree on something is all."

Captain Stewart snorted. "Sounded more like a lovers' spat. If you two make me regret looking the other way while you have a relationship, I promise that I'm going to make both of you regret it more." When Dane looked like he wanted to argue, their boss jabbed a finger in his direction. "Don't test me, Dane, or I'll have you transferred to a new station by tomorrow."

Dane clenched his jaw. He stared at the captain for a long time as if wondering whether the man was bluffing. After a moment, Dane shook his head and walked out. A few seconds later, she heard him stomping down the steps.

Stewart looked at Lexi, his expression hard. "That goes for you, too. I'm not putting up with this crap. Understood?"

"Yes, sir."

Giving Lexi a nod, he turned and left the

locker room, closing the door behind him.

Tears stinging her eyes, Lexi turned and walked down the row of lockers until she got to hers. She didn't know whether she wanted to cry because she was hurt by what Dane had said or because she was so freaking pissed at him.

She was taking off her shoes when she heard the door open. She quickly wiped the few tears that had escaped to slide down her face and spun around, thinking Dane had come back for another round. But it was Kate Fairchild, one of the female firefighters on the shift. While she and Kate had met when Lexi transferred to Station 58, they were becoming fast friends.

Lexi peeled off her damp T-shirt. "I guess everyone in the station heard Dane and me, huh?"

Kate gave her a sympathetic smile. "Actually, I think they heard you guys down at the next station."

Lexi groaned. "Great."

Kate sat down on the long bench in front of the lockers. Slender with long blond hair and green eyes, she had that quintessential girl next door look about her.

"I didn't know Dane was such a sexist jerk," Lexi said, pushing down her pants and stepping out of them.

"I don't think he means to be," Kate said. "I think he cares about you."

Lexi angrily shoved her wet clothes in the laundry bag she kept in the bottom of her locker. "Then he'd respect me enough to let me do my job." She glanced over her shoulder at Kate. "Have any of the guys in DF&R ever called you out because they didn't think a woman can do the job?"

Kate nodded. "A few times. I hate to say it, but it's one of the hazards of being a woman in a male-oriented, macho occupation."

Lexi tossed her soggy sports bra and panties on top of the other wet clothes in the laundry bag then pulled on new underwear and a fresh uniform.

"Why do guys have to be that way?" she asked as she sat down on the bed beside Kate and pulled on her shoes.

Kate shrugged. "In some cases, men are simply wired at the genetic level to protect women. In other cases, it's a blatant preconceived notion that women aren't capable of doing the job."

Lexi remembered what Skye had said about being grateful she'd found a man who believed in her and helped her get where she wanted to be. She'd thought Dane might be that man for her.

"For what it's worth, Dane has always been fair with me and the other female firefighters in the station," Kate said quietly.

Lexi wasn't sure if that made her feel better or worse. "Do you think getting involved with him was a mistake?"

Kate gave her a small smile. "You're the only one who can answer that question."

That wasn't much help. But Kate was right. She was going to have to decide if Dane was worth it. Despite how much she was beginning to care about him, right now, she wasn't so sure.

* * * * *

Dane should have known Jax would follow him. No sooner had he walked outside to cool off than his friend caught up with him. Even though the torrential rain had stopped right after the Dallas PD detective had shown up to talk to Lexi and Trent, the ground was still soggy.

"What was that all about?" Jax demanded.

"Nothing," Dane barked as he strode over to the picnic tables set up near the grills along the side of the building.

Jax kept pace with him. "It didn't sound like nothing to me."

When Dane didn't answer—or stop—Jax grabbed his arm and jerked him to a halt. "What the hell is your problem?"

"My problem is that Lexi almost got herself killed tonight." Dane's gut clenched thinking about it. "I told her that she shouldn't have taken a risk like that, and she took it the wrong way."

"Did she?" Jax said. "Because it seems to me like she took it exactly the right way."

"What the hell is that supposed to mean?"

"If Trent had been the one crawling out there on the top of that car, would you be berating him for being reckless?"

The question caught Dane by surprise, and when he opened his mouth to answer it, nothing came out. He ground his jaw. "That's different."

Jax lifted a brow. "And that's where the problem starts. Because it's not different, except for the minor fact that you're not sleeping with Trent. At least not that I'm aware of."

Despite how pissed off—and terrified he still was when he thought of what could have happened to Lexi tonight—Dane couldn't help chuckling. "No, I'm not sleeping with Trent. His bunk is kinda close to mine upstairs, though, so maybe that counts." He shook his head. "You know what I'm talking about. It's hard as hell seeing the woman I care about so much doing something so frigging crazy, that's all."

"Maybe that's something you should have thought about before deciding to date a woman who happens to be a paramedic in the DF&R," Jax pointed out. "Paramedics frequently risk their lives when they go on calls. It comes with the job description."

Dane sighed. "I know that. I hadn't realized it would be so damn tough to handle."

"You think it's hard on you, imagine being in Lexi's shoes watching you run into burning buildings day after day."

Dane definitely hadn't thought about it that way. In fact, he hadn't been thinking at all. That wasn't so new. If the situation with his sister had taught himself anything, it was that he tended to open his mouth before engaging his head. And it usually came back to bite him in the ass.

He ran his hand through his hair with a sigh. "I guess I should go apologize."

"Probably," Jax agreed. "But before you do that, you need to take a step back and ask yourself what you're going to do the next time she does something dangerous."

Dane didn't answer. The idea of something happening to Lexi was enough to make him break out in a cold sweat.

"I don't know," he finally admitted.

"Well, you need to figure it out," Jax said. "Because it's going to happen again. And if you can't deal with that, then there's no reason to apologize to Lexi. You can't say you're sorry while knowing you're going to blow up again the next time she has to put herself in danger for her job. It would be disingenuous."

"Disingenuous?" Dane arched a brow. "Anyone ever mention your Doctor Drew imitation sucks? Shouldn't you be trying to give me some advice on how to deal with this situation?"

Jax didn't even crack a smile. "I am giving you advice—you're not listening. Lexi works a job that can be dangerous, like yours. If you're not ready to accept that, maybe it's a good thing this argument happened now, before you and Lexi get too deeply involved."

Dane didn't bother mentioning it was too late for that. He and Lexi were already deeply involved. At least, as far as he was concerned. He supposed he couldn't really answer for Lexi, especially after the jackass he'd made of himself tonight.

"Let me ask you something," Jax said. "What if Lexi came to you and said she didn't like the idea of you being a firefighter anymore. How would you handle that?"

"I never said she should quit her job," Dane protested.

"Didn't you?"

His friend didn't wait for an answer, but turned and headed back into the station. Dane stayed where he was, thinking about what Jax had said. Dane definitely wouldn't have taken too kindly to Lexi calling him out for doing his job or implying that he should quit. He hadn't meant to imply that Lexi couldn't do her job—or needed to walk away from it—but Jax had been right. That was the way it had come out. At the same time, it was damn tough seeing Lexi in danger. Even worse when it was danger she'd voluntarily put herself in.

What the hell was he supposed to do?

No matter how long he stood out there, he still didn't have an answer. He knew one thing for sure. He wasn't walking away from Lexi, not over something like this.

Figuring this situation wouldn't get better with age, he headed inside. He didn't know exactly what he was going to say, but he needed to talk to Lexi anyway.

He was still fifteen feet away from the station doors when he heard the sound of running feet and one of the trucks start up. At the same time, the alarm went off, and the red light out on the curb began strobing, warning drivers on the street that a vehicle was pulling out. A moment later, Rescue 58 rolled out the door, Lexi behind the wheel.

Dane didn't even have time to wave, much less tell her to be careful, before she and Trent turned onto the street, taillights disappearing into the darkness.

He jogged into the vehicle bay in case the station's other trucks had been called out, too, but there was no one around. That meant this was an EMS roll-out only.

Dane told himself that was a good thing, that if the situation only required paramedics it wouldn't be dangerous. But his gut called bullshit on that. There were plenty of scary situations paramedics could get themselves into all on their own.

Shit.

Jax was right. He was going to have to come to grips with this or what he had going with Lexi would fall apart before it truly got started.

* * * * *

"Sorry about you and Dane," Trent said quietly as they sped down I-75 toward University Park.

The area around Park City and Southern Methodist University was usually serviced jointly by Station 27 and the University Park Fire Department, so it was well outside the usual Station 58 response zone, but between the rain and those idiot street racers, half the rescue vehicles in the city were out on call at the moment. Division had sent her and Trent out on the call about an injured pedestrian simply because they were the closest crew available.

"There's nothing for you to be sorry about." The rain started again, and Lexi flicked on the wipers as she guided the truck off I-75 and onto the Central Expressway. "I knew there was a chance that dating a firefighter in my own station might blow up in my face."

Trent sighed. "Okay, so maybe sorry isn't the right word. I know how frustrated you are right now, but you need to pull back a second and realize nothing has been said that can't be unsaid, and nothing has been blown up that can't be put back together."

Okay, that wasn't something you'd usually expect a guy to say. Then again, Trent didn't seem like a guy ruled by his inner caveman. Unlike Dane.

She glanced at him as she pulled off the expressway onto the Northwest Highway. "You seriously think this is something Dane and I can get past? He called me out in front of the whole station for doing my job."

Trent glanced at the incident report before answering. "You're seriously ready to walk away from a guy you're clearly into because he didn't know how to put into words how scared he was for you?"

She started to say something snarky about the fact that it wasn't Dane's job to worry about her, but the words hung up in her throat. She knew what it was like to be scared for someone. Heck, she'd been freaked out a few days ago when Jax and Tory had pulled Dane out of that burning apartment complex.

"Me being all observant and crap, I see I've struck a nerve," Trent said sarcastically. "Look, I won't go all sexist on you and attempt to say women are better at hiding their feelings when it comes to concerns over their lover's occupation. That's BS. But I can confidently say that most men suck at it. Flat-out, Dane saw you doing something that suddenly made him realize he's building a relationship with a woman who does a job as dangerous as his, and it freaked him out."

"Shouldn't he have figured that out before?" she asked.

Trent shrugged. "You'd think so. But like my getting into a relationship with a woman that spends more time on a plane than she does on the ground, most of the time we don't think beyond the issue of finding a woman we click with. It's that single-focus caveman thing that's wired into our DNA. Dane is falling for you—which is a great thing—but now he's finally figuring out his relationship is going to come with a few speed bumps along the way, and I don't think he was ready for it."

She sighed, knowing deep down that Trent was right. Maybe she shouldn't have reacted the way she had, but she hadn't exactly been in a good frame of mind. She'd been riding on an adrenaline high after saving someone's life, and lashed out without thought.

"So you think it's on me to help Dane work through this?" she finally said.

"It's on both of you," Trent said. "If you and Dane aren't willing to put a little effort into dealing with the first frigging obstacle that appears in the road, maybe this isn't the relationship for you. Hell, maybe relationships in general aren't for you."

O-kay. She shot him a sharp look. "That's a little blunt, don't you think?"

Trent chuckled. "Maybe. But if you can't be blunt with your friends, who can you be blunt with?"

Lexi shook her head with a laugh. Trent was right. If she and Dane couldn't handle something this simple, how were they ever going to handle the hard stuff life was bound to throw their way?

She slowed at the sight of flashing blue lights near the park off Hillcrest. Trent checked the incident sheet and confirmed this was where they were supposed to be. But as they pulled up, neither of them saw an injured pedestrian anywhere. All she saw was a police officer standing in front of his patrol car.

"Where's our injured pedestrian?" Lexi asked the cop as she and Trent got out of the truck.

The officer pointed at the opposite side of the street. "We got here a few minutes ago to find a homeless guy with a busted up leg sitting in the grass over there. He said some crazy drivers slammed into the cars parked by the curb, hitting him in the process before speeding off. The guy's leg looked pretty bad, but he said he wasn't going to hang around in the rain any longer and started walking south down this side of Hillcrest. My partner is following him."

Lexi thanked him then she and Trent got back in their rescue truck and started down Hillcrest. They ended up finding their patient a quarter mile down the road, patiently limping along the sidewalk, a police officer at his side.

As they got out and approached, she took in the injured man's worn but expensive looking camouflage jacket. She'd been around enough military types to recognize a GORE-TEX jacket. This guy was probably a veteran, and while he might look rough around the edges, she didn't think he was more than twenty-eight- or twenty-nine-years-old. There was blood seeping through the leg of the man's dirty jeans and based on how bad he was hobbling, Lexi was confident it was broken.

Lexi passed the police officer, falling into step with the injured man and giving him a smile. "Hi there. I'm Lexi and I'm a paramedic with Dallas Fire and Rescue. Your leg seems to be causing you a little trouble. Do you mind if I take a look?"

When the man eyed her suspiciously, she smiled at him again. After a few steps, he nodded then stopped, letting her take his hand and lead him to the back of the rescue truck.

"What's your name?" she asked the bearded man as she and Trent got him on a gurney.

"Jessie."

Her lips curved. "Well, Jessie, we're going to fix you right up."

Jessie nodded, but then held up a hand and shook his head the moment Trent picked up scissors to slice open his jeans. "These are the only pants I got."

Trent glanced at her, lifting a questioning brow.

"Jessie, we won't be able to help you if we can't take a look at your leg," she said gently. "I promise I'll make sure you get a new pair of pants. Okay?"

Jessie hesitated for a moment, but then nodded and relaxed back on the gurney. One look at his leg after Trent sliced open his jeans told her it was definitely broken. Lexi couldn't believe he'd walked as far as he had.

"What happened?" she asked Jessie as they tended to his leg.

"It was Ismael Montero and those damn asshole buddies of his. They race around here like they own the frigging city," Jessie grumbled, his gray eyes meeting hers. "I was walking past those cars back there, and they damn near crushed me. I'm going over to his shop after you fix up my leg so I can kick the effing tar out of him and all his stupid friends."

Lexi exchanged looks with Trent.

"You know the people who have been racing around Dallas in those souped-up cars?" she asked Jessie.

The man eyed her as she cleaned his leg, barely flinching as she gently wiped blood out of the multiple lacerations.

"Of course I know them." He snorted. "Everyone knows them. It's Ismael. He runs a chop shop over on Northhaven."

"Would you mind if I pass that information along to a detective I know?" she asked. "Those guys nearly killed a woman over on the Lyndon Johnson Freeway earlier tonight."

The man shrugged. "Go ahead. As long as I get a chance to kick his ass first."

Lexi shook her head. "I'm afraid your ass-kicking adventure might have to be put on hold for a couple of days. Your leg is broken and is going to have to be set and put in a cast."

Jessie looked like he would have complained, but Lexi hit him with a big smile, which ended the arguing before it started. Huh. Maybe she should have used that one on Dane.

As Trent strapped the gurney in and prepped Jessie to move, Lexi headed around to the front of the truck, taking Detective Maxwell's card out of her wallet as she went.

Chapter Eleven

DANE TOOK A deep breath and blew it out slowly. He'd been standing outside Lexi's door for the past five minutes trying to get the courage to ring the doorbell. Damn, he was pathetic.

He wanted to blame it on the last two sleepless nights he'd had, but in reality it was plain old fear. It wasn't his fault. He hadn't been able to talk to her Tuesday night after their fight because the call she'd gone on had kept her out until nearly two and when she'd gotten back, she'd made a beeline for the female sleeping quarters. He'd hoped to see her after their shift ended, but she'd already left by the time he'd come downstairs".

He could have stopped by to see her yesterday—or even called her—but the truth was, he'd chickened out. He had to talk to her today or face her tomorrow at work without getting any of this mess straightened out. He definitely didn't want to do that.

Telling himself to stop being such a damn coward, he rang the doorbell.

He hoped Melinda wasn't the one who answered. That would be awkward. Hell, Lexi's roommate probably already knew all the stupid stuff he'd said and probably would kick him in the balls for being an asshole to her friend.

When the door opened, he was relieved to see Lexi standing there. She had on a pair of yoga pants and a tank top, her silky, dark hair hanging down her back. Her blue eyes were guarded, like she wasn't sure what he was going to say. Truthfully, he wasn't sure what he was going to say either. He only hoped it wasn't something else stupid. That was a distinct possibility since he'd never been very good with words—unless you considered pissing off the most important people in his life to be a talent. In that case, he was a master of the English language.

He cleared his throat. "Can I come in so we can talk?"

She regarded him in silence for a moment then stepped back. "Yeah."

He stepped inside and waited while she closed the door then followed her over to the couch. The TV was on with the sound down low. It looked like some kind of news special report.

"Did you see the news this morning?" Lexi asked, gesturing to the TV as she sat down on the sofa and tucked her feet under her.

Dane took a seat on the adjacent couch, careful to leave a little distance between them. "No. Something interesting on it?"

"The police caught those people who have been running the street racing events all over town," she said. "Detective Maxwell was on a few minutes ago talking about the arrest. Apparently, it was nothing more than a big game of I-dare-you. Twenty car wrecks and multiple serious injuries over a four-day period for a silly game."

Didn't make a whole hell of a lot of sense, did it? "At least they caught the jackasses before someone died. That's the important thing." He glanced toward the bedrooms "Is Melinda here?"

Lexi shook her head. "No. She's been working nearly back-to-back shifts at the hospital the past couple of days. She called this morning and said she was going to crash for a few hours in the nurse's lounge then work another shift today."

Damn, Melinda's schedule sounded worse than a firefighter's. He was glad they were alone in the apartment, though. It would make it easier to say what he had to say.

"I guess I should start with an apology," he said quietly. "I was a complete ass, and what I said to you at the station was totally out of bounds."

Dane didn't know what he expected her to say, but all he got was a nod and an expectant look. He guessed that was her way of telling him to keep going.

"I never intended to imply that I didn't think you could do your job," he continued. "Or that you were foolish or reckless or anything else that you may have taken from my crappy choice of words."

"Then what were you implying?" she asked simply.

He shrugged. "That's it. I wasn't implying anything. I wasn't even thinking. I was reacting to seeing you climb out of the sunroof of that car as it hung there on the edge of the overpass. When I realized how close to being killed you'd come, my head shut down and everything that came out of my mouth was driven by pure fear."

Lexi considered his words. "I can understand that, but if you had the chance to go back and do it all over again, would you do anything differently?"

It was his turn to ponder her words. "Knowing what I know now? Knowing how much I hurt and embarrassed you? Yeah, I'd do it all differently."

Dane paused before continuing, wanting to make sure everything came out right this time. He was still as terrified as he'd been that night they'd argued at the station, but for a completely different reason. This time, he was worried he was going to say something that would drive Lexi away forever. He couldn't live with himself if that happened.

"For one thing, I'd tell you that what I

saw was the bravest, most selfless thing I'd ever witnessed. You were amazing," he said. "And as soon as I finished, I would have pulled you into my arms and hugged you and told you that I'd never been so scared in my life. That in all the times I'd risked my life in a fire or some other rescue scenario, I never feared death like I did at that moment. Because you're more important to me than anything, even my own life."

Dane wanted to tell her he loved her right then, because he did. He'd come to that realization the other night on the overpass, but hadn't admitted it to himself until this morning. As much as he wanted to pour his heart out to Lexi, saying those three all-important words while they were trying to work through an issue as great as this one would be too much like emotional blackmail.

So he said the next best thing.

"Lexi, I know I screwed up and said some pretty crappy stuff the other night, but I can't stand the idea of walking away from what we have. I need you to know that I'm willing to keep working on this. I hope you're willing to let me."

Tears filled her eyes, and for a moment he feared she was going to tell him it was too late. That she'd already decided to move on.

"I want to believe you," she said softly. "But how are you going to handle it the next time I have to do something you think is too dangerous? I don't get put into life and death situations as often as you do as a firefighter, but it will happen at some point."

He swallowed hard. "I'll never get comfortable with the idea of seeing you in danger, but I've accepted it's something I'll have to deal with. I know it's part of a package deal, like my being a firefighter is for you. I need you to promise that you'll always remember there's someone who needs you to come home every day."

Lexi gazed at him for a long time, tears running down her face. It took everything in Dane not to close the distance between them, wrap his arms around her, and kiss them away.

Please don't let it be too little, too late.

But then she got up and came over to sit beside him. A moment later, she leaned in to kiss him, and if her lips were a little wet with tears, he wasn't going to complain.

"I promise," she said when she pulled away, her voice barely above a whisper as she looked him straight in the eye. "But you have to make the same promise as well. Because you're very important to me, and I don't want to think about what life would be like without you in it."

Dane smiled, relief flooding through him. "I promise."

Lexi kissed him again then rested her forehead against his with a groan. "I want to spend the rest of the day kissing you like this, but I told the patient Trent and I dropped off at the hospital the other night that I'd stop by and see him. Do you want to come with me then afterward we can come back here and hang out?"

"Actually, I promised Jax and Skye I'd stop by and help set up some stuff for the wedding tomorrow," he said. "But I'd love to hang out after that. If you're sure it's okay?"

Her lips curved into a smile. "It's definitely okay. I know we're both probably still a little gun shy over everything that was said, but I want us to get back to where we were before. Spending our day off together is a good start."

They agreed to meet back at her place at four then Dane walked her to her car. Before she got in, Lexi pulled him down for a long, slow kiss. "I'm glad we worked stuff out. It's only been a day since we saw each other, but I really missed you."

Dane knew exactly what she meant.

* * * * *

Lexi was still smiling as she walked into the hospital. Despite her conversation with Trent, she'd avoided Dane at the station the other night then left as soon as her shift was over. She'd almost called him a dozen times since, but they needed to talk about things face to face. After tossing and turning for the past two nights, she'd gotten up that morning intending to go over to Dane's place since he obviously wasn't going to make the first move. But then he'd shown up at her door.

She'd wanted to drag him into her

apartment and kiss him until they were both out of breath, but she'd restrained herself. The wait had been worth it. The things Dane said to her today had made her cry for a completely different reason than they had the other night. His words had made her heart do somersaults in her chest.

Lexi didn't care that she and Dane had only been dating a little while. She was in love with him, plain and simple. Like Skye had said, who someone fell for or how fast didn't have to follow any rules.

Stepping off the elevator, Lexi made her way to the nurse's station. The blond woman handling the desk looked up from her computer as she approached. Lexi explained that she was a paramedic with DF&R then asked if the nurse knew which rooms Debra Wallace and Jessie Strickland were in. She'd only promised Jessie she'd visit, but since she was there, she wanted to check on Debra, too.

The nurse tapped on her keyboard, then stared at the computer screen. After a moment, she shook her head. "I don't see room numbers for either patient."

Lexi frowned. "Were they released already?"

The nurse typed something else into the computer. "It doesn't show that they were released." More typing. "That's odd."

"What's odd?"

"The records don't say anything about their status at all. A few notes about insurance and what their injuries were, then nothing."

Lexi took her cell phone from her purse and dialed Melinda, She hated bothering her friend, but she couldn't shake the funny feeling building up in her stomach. It was silly, but after what had happened to Wayne last week, she had to know.

"Hey, Melinda," she said when her friend answered. "I'm at the nurse's station on the fifth floor. Can you come up here for a minute?"

"Yeah. I'll be right there."

Melinda looked like crap when she stepped off the elevator. No shock there. With the exception of a few catnaps here and there, her friend had been working for the better part of the past forty-eight hours.

"You look terrible," Lexi said.

"Nice to see you, too," Melinda responded with none of her usual spark. "There's a flu bug going around and half the nurses are down with it. Everyone who can walk is pulling multiple shifts. What dragged you down here on your day off?"

"I came to see the two patients Trent and I treated Tuesday night—the woman from the car on the overpass and the homeless veteran the street racers hit."

Melinda stared at her like she had no idea what Lexi was talking about then her eyes widened. "That was Tuesday night? I'd completely lost all track of what day of the week it was."

"Can you help me figure out where they are?" Lexi asked. "I assume they were released, but I'd like to get addresses so I can go see them and make sure they're doing okay. I'm especially worried about Jessie. I'm not sure that guy has a place to go."

Melinda walked around the desk and checked the computer database, but she didn't learn anything more than the other nurse. "With so many people out, housekeeping stuff like putting information into the database isn't taking priority right now. Let me see if I can find the hardcopy files."

Her friend disappeared into a big room behind the nurse's station then came back a few minutes later, two files in her hand and a glum look on her face.

Lexi's stomach plummeted. "What's wrong?"

"I'm sorry, Lexi, but neither patient made it," Melinda said gently.

She shook her head. "That can't be right. They only had minor injuries—a broken leg and lacerations. There's no way they could have died from those."

Melinda set the files down on the desk and opened each of them. "According to the doctor's notes, Jessie Strickland died of an aneurysm brought on by overuse of methamphetamine. Debra Wallace had a congenital heart defect that led to a heart attack."

Lexi glanced at the files. Sure enough,

that's what they said. "That can't be right. I hooked Debra up to a cardiac monitor and ran an EKG before the other team of paramedics brought her in, and she had no arrhythmia of any kind. Jessie didn't show a single symptom associated with an aneurysm or meth use."

Melinda's eyes were sad. "Honey, I know what you did to save those two, but they still didn't make it. Sometimes, that happens."

Lexi stood there, emotions warring inside her. Sorrow, depression, confusion, and anger all fighting to see which one would come out on top. Finally, anger won out.

"Who was the ER doctor who treated them? I want him—or her—to look me in the face and tell me how Jessie and Debra died."

Her friend hesitated for a moment then sighed and flipped through the files until she found the name Lexi was looking for. "It was the same doctor in both cases—Dr. Harold Patton."

Lexi frowned. "Wasn't he the same doctor on duty the night Wayne Moore died?"

"Yes," Melinda said. "But that's not shocking. Patton works more shifts than I do. He's here practically every night."

Melinda might not think it was strange, but it seemed damn suspicious to Lexi. "Is he here now? I want to talk to him."

It was obviously from the look on Melinda's face she thought that was a bad idea, but her friend finally nodded. "You can probably find him in the doctor's lounge on the second floor, trying to grab a nap."

"Thanks."

Melinda opened her mouth to say something, but Lexi didn't hang around to listen. Instead, she hurried to the elevator. She was going to find Patton and get some answers as to how two perfectly healthy people had died so suddenly.

By the time she got to the doctor's lounge, however, some of her fire had dissipated as she realized she had no idea exactly what she was going to say to the man. She pushed open the door anyway, hoping something would come to mind.

The room was dark and, for a moment, she thought it was empty. Then she saw the man sitting on the couch staring at the wall on the far side of the room.

"Dr. Patton?"

"What do you want?" he demanded, not looking at her. "I told the nurses I didn't want to be bothered unless there was an emergency."

She walked into the room and turned on the light.

Patton held up one hand, shielding his eyes from the sudden brightness. "Shit. What'd you do that for?"

Lexi ignored the question. "Dr. Patton, my name is Lexi Fletcher. I'm a paramedic with DF&R. I brought in two patients Tuesday night, and now they're both dead. I was hoping you could tell me what happened."

He leaned his head back on the couch

and rested his forearm across his eyes. "Their hearts stopped beating, I assume. That's the way death usually occurs."

A shiver went through her at his words. She shook it off and stepped closer. "I looked at Debra Wallace's EKG myself before I brought her in, and there was no arrhythmia like her record suggests."

She would have explained that Jessie Strickland showed no signs of drug use, or impending aneurysm, but a low, sarcastic laugh cut her off.

"That's funny," Patton sneered. "A paramedic telling me I can't read a heart trace."

"I was pre-med in college—"

"Fucking goody for you." He jumped to his feet so fast, she took a startled step back. "Why don't you come back and talk to me again after you finish med school and your residency? Then, maybe I'll give a shit about what you have to say."

Lexi would have told Patton what he could do with his arrogant attitude, but she was too shocked by what she saw in his eyes. They were dilated as far as she'd ever seen, almost as large as his entire iris. His dark-blond hair was soaked with sweat and his face was pale as a ghost.

Either it was speed, or maybe some kind of opiate like oxycodone. Either way, Dr. Patton was high as a freaking kite. She couldn't believe none of the hospital staff had noticed.

"Now, if you'll excuse me, I have more important things to do than talk to you."

She watched in shock as he stormed from the room. Crap. The hospital had a drug addict working in their ER, one who had almost certainly let two people—three, if Wayne was also a victim—die due to negligence. But how did she prove it?

* * * * *

"What's he's saying?" Lexi whispered to Dane, who was listening intently on his cell phone to Detective Maxwell.

They were alone in the station's dayroom, so there was no chance of them being overheard. Dane gave her a nod.

"Hold on, Logan. I'm putting you on speaker so Lexi can hear."

He thumbed the speaker button on his iPhone then held it so they could both listen. They'd been waiting all day for the DPD detective to call, and Dane knew Lexi was as eager as he was to hear what the cop had to say.

When Dane had met up with Lexi at her apartment last night, she'd been waiting for him at the door. He'd taken one look at her face and immediately realized something was wrong. It had taken her a while to get it all out, but as soon as she had, he knew why she was so freaked. Not only was there a doctor at the local hospital getting high while on duty, there was also a good chance his drug use had ended up getting three people killed—maybe more. Stuff like this wasn't supposed to happen, not in a city like Dallas.

Unfortunately, they had absolutely no proof, unless you counted Patton's dilated pupils and pale, sweaty face. But the thought of not believing Lexi never entered Dane's mind. Not only did he trust her medical judgement, he trusted her instincts, too.

The first thing he'd done was call the station and tell them to download the memory card on Rescue 58's cardiac monitor. Then he agreed they had to tell someone—fast.

They'd gone back and forth between calling the cops and formally reporting their suspicions to the hospital. Finally, they opted for the police. With nothing to go on, neither one of them could imagine the hospital taking their accusations seriously.

They'd called Logan Maxwell because they didn't really know who else to turn to. They figured, if nothing else, the guy owed Lexi a favor for the tip that had helped Logan take down the street racing crew. Logan hadn't made any promises, but had told them he'd look into the situation. At the minimum, he could poke around and see if he picked up any rumors on the street about Patton's drug use.

"I have to admit, I didn't think I'd find anything when I started snooping," Logan said now. "But I think you two may have stumbled onto something bigger than even you imagined."

"You already found something about Patton's drug use?" Lexi asked.

"The drug use didn't take long to confirm, at least informally," Logan said. "You'd think a doctor would get his drugs from the hospital, but I've talked to a number of local dealers who admit to selling Patton a medicine cabinet full of opiate-based drugs."

"I'm sure he's probably stealing them from the hospital, too," Lexi said. "But if he's using heavily, I doubt he can skim enough to keep up with his habit without someone catching onto what he's doing."

"No doubt," Logan agreed. "But while confirming Patton is on drugs was useful—and will certainly get us a warrant to search his home and locker at the hospital at some point—it's not nearly as interesting as the fact that I can't find the bodies of those three deceased patients."

Dane frowned, sure he'd heard wrong. He glanced at Lexi to see her sitting there with a stunned look as well. Okay, apparently, he'd heard right after all.

"What do you mean, you couldn't find the bodies?" Dane asked.

"I can't find them because they're missing. I stopped by the hospital this morning to see if they'd requested an autopsy on the three patients. Hospitals rarely do that in those cases where it's deemed natural causes, but it turned out they had, something to do with the fact that the deaths followed possible criminal activities—a fire and two street racing accidents. The only problem? While the hospital showed me transfer paperwork, the medical examiner insists the bodies never arrived at the Forensic Institute."

"How is that possible?" Lexi asked. "Bodies aren't socks. You don't lose them."

"I agree," Logan said. "If this was one body missing, I'd assume it was a clerical error like an idiot filling out the transfer paperwork wrong and sending the body to a funeral home instead of the ME's offices. But with three of them missing, that's not a clerical error. There's something weird going on."

"Logan, do you think there's a chance Patton is selling the bodies on the black market for parts?" Lexi asked. "I mean, other than the injuries that supposedly killed them all three of the people we treated were healthy."

"Damn, I never even thought of that," Logan said. "I've been working under the assumption Patton killed them because he was negligent and they're missing because the doctor is trying to clean up any evidence of his mistakes. Your theory is as feasible—and a whole lot scarier."

"It might be even more likely," Dane said, a sudden uncomfortable thought coming to him. "It can't be a coincidence that all three of the people who died on his watch happen to be people with no direct family members around to ask questions."

Logan was quiet for a long time. "Huh. I didn't realize that. So, either we're dealing with an incompetent drug addict, or a serial killer. Either way, I gotta start pushing the warrants as fast as possible. I hope to have something in a few hours."

They talked a little while longer, with Logan promising to keep them up to speed on his investigation before he hung up.

"Do you think Patton really targeted these three people because they had no family?" Lexi asked.

Dane shook his head. "Who can guess how a psycho thinks? The thing that scares me is how do we know he hasn't done this before? We're not the only fire station that uses the hospital. There could be a lot more than three deaths involved here."

"Crap," Lexi muttered. "You're right."

Dane opened his mouth to say something else when the station alarm went off. It was quickly followed by the announcement, "Engine 58, Truck 58, Rescue 58, residential structure fire at 155 Plymouth."

He and Lexi jumped to their feet and ran for the vehicle bay.

"Be careful out there," she called to him as she headed toward her rescue vehicle.

"You, too," he said as he reached for his turnout gear and started getting dressed.

He slipped his feet into his boots and quickly pulled up the heavy pants then looped the suspenders over his shoulders without even thinking about it. That was probably a good thing since his mind was swimming at the possibility that this fire might send someone to the hospital staffed with a frigging serial killer.

Chapter Twelve

AS LEXI AND Trent pulled up in front of the hospital, her heart was thumping a thousand miles an hour, and it had nothing to do with the five-year-old kid they had in the back with first degree burns to his legs and hands. Instead, she was freaked out over the possibility of having Dr. Patton get anywhere near their patient. She'd left half a dozen messages with Logan, praying the detective had already arrested the doctor, but the detective hadn't called back yet. She knew it was wishful thinking to hope the legal system worked that fast.

Lexi had told Trent everything she knew about Patton on the drive to the hospital. He'd been shocked as hell, but he'd agreed to help her, first by trying to get dispatch to let them take the kid to a different hospital claiming there was excessive traffic, then promising to stay with the little boy until the parents arrived when the dispatcher refused to reroute them.

"This isn't like the other patients," Trent reminded her. "This kid has family to keep an eye on Patton. He's not going to try anything with witnesses around."

Lexi knew he was right. Wayne, Debra, and Jessie had all been on their own with no one to make a fuss when they turned up dead. But that still didn't make her feel any better, especially since they were still only guessing when it came to how the doctor chose his victims. She didn't feel good about the fact that the three victims they knew about had all died at night, well after visiting hours. The kid would be as alone then as all the others.

So when she saw Melinda in the hallway leading to the ER examination area, she pulled her roommate aside. Melinda hadn't come home last night until late and Lexi had left early, so she hadn't been able to tell her friend anything about Patton yet. That needed to change.

"Is Patton working tonight?" she asked urgently.

Her roommate nodded. "Yeah. The guy practically lives here. Why?"

"Have you seen the police talking to him recently?" Lexi prodded.

Melinda looked at her in obvious confusion. "What? No. Why would the police be talking to him? He's a rude asshole, to be sure, but I don't think they can arrest you for that."

Lexi sighed. That really wasn't what she'd wanted to hear. She grabbed her friend's arm and pulled her farther away from the crowd of people streaming through the ER.

"Melinda, I don't have time to get into the details, but I'm pretty sure Patton is addicted to pain meds. The police are currently investigating him in the deaths of those three patients I brought in. It's also possible that he stole the bodies to hide the evidence of what he did to them. Or, worse, to sell their body parts."

Melinda gaped at her.

Lexi would have liked to give her friend a moment to process that bombshell before hurrying on, but there wasn't any time for that.

"The police should be showing up soon to arrest Patton," she continued. "But until that happens, you have to be on him like a shadow. Don't let him give anyone any drugs unless you know what it is."

"What? Lexi, I'm a nurse. How am I going to stop a doctor from giving a drug to a patient?"

"I don't know, but you're going to have to figure out something," Lexi said urgently. "We can't let Patton kill anyone else."

Melinda took a deep breath then nodded. "I'll do what I can, but what we really need to do is get a senior doctor involved. Someone who has the authority, knowledge—and the nerve to stop Patton if he tries something."

Lexi wasn't sure if that was a good idea. What if one of Patton's fellow doctors asked why the police were investigating him? Who knew what Patton would do then?

But they had to try something.

"Is there a doctor on duty that you trust implicitly?"

"Dr. Lambert," Melinda said without hesitation. "He's the best doctor we have. If you tell him what's going on, he'll help."

Lexi nodded, remembering their meeting the other day. "Where is he now?"

Melinda gave her directions to an office complex on the second floor. "He runs his research projects out of there, so you might have to look around in some of the labs."

Lexi turned and ran for the stairwell. She found Dr. Lambert in one of the labs down the hall from his office. He was studying a rack filled with test tubes and medicine vials, humming to himself as he wrote down some notes. On the table beside them was a small cage with two mice in it.

She knocked on the open door then walked in. "Dr. Lambert, may I talk to you? It's urgent."

He turned, a warm smile spreading across his face. "Ms. Fletcher, isn't it? The paramedic?"

Lexi nodded, relieved he recognized her. That might help when it came to believing the insane story she was about to tell him.

"That's me," she said. "Melinda introduced us."

"I remember." His smile broadened. "What can I help you with?"

"I think one of the doctors at the hospital is murdering patients," she said without preemption.

Okay, considering the alarm that crossed Dr. Lambert's face, she probably could have come up with a better way to start this whole thing. But it was out now.

"Perhaps you had better start from the beginning," he said in a tone that was far calmer than Lexi would have expected. "This sounds like something I should definitely hear."

Lexi nodded, telling Dr. Lambert everything she knew as he turned his attention back to the test tubes in the rack. She tried not to talk too quickly, but she was intensely aware Patton was downstairs right this second, likely looking at the kid she and Trent had brought in. There wasn't a lot of time to do this.

Dr. Lambert must have realized it, too, because his eyes widened in concern. "You're sure the police will be here soon to look for the missing bodies?"

"I assume they'll take Dr. Patton into custody first, but then they'll probably start questioning all the people who are normally involved with handling the bodies here at the hospital," she said. "At some point, I'm sure they'll find someone who knows something."

"I'm sure." Sighing, Dr. Lambert set down the clipboard he'd been holding and picked up a syringe from the table. He glanced at her as he took out a medicine vial from a drawer and plunged the tip of the needle into the rubber stopper then filled the syringe with the clear liquid. "Why don't you go back down to the ER? I'll meet you there shortly."

Lexi nodded and started for the door. She took two steps then stopped and turned back to him. "Thank you for believing me."

"Actually. I'm the one who should be thanking you for the warning."

She opened her mouth to tell him she was simply doing her job when she felt a sharp jab in her left arm. Startled, she flinched and tried to pull away, but Dr. Lambert grabbed her elbow and held on tightly. She looked down and saw the barrel of the syringe he'd filled pressed against her triceps.

She jerked her head up to demand an explanation when a wave of dizziness washed over her and everything went fuzzy, making it impossible to get the words out. Suddenly, her legs felt like Jell-O.

Crap. She'd been drugged.

She was vaguely aware of Lambert dragging her back into his lab and closing the door behind them. She shoved feebly at the hand holding her arm, but her muscles were complete mush. Humming to himself, Lambert lowered to the floor as her legs gave out. Then everything went black.

* * * * *

"Have you found her yet?" Dane demanded as he met up with Trent and Logan in the middle of the hallway leading to the ER.

His gut clenched when both men shook their heads. He cursed, torn between punching the wall and letting out a string of even more colorful expletives. Instead, he resisted the urge to do either and took a deep breath.

"Tell me everything again," he said to Trent. "When was the last time anyone saw Lexi?"

Dane had still been working clean-up at the residential house fire, when Trent called him to say Lexi was missing. Dane had been so busy fighting the fire, he hadn't even realized Lexi had left to take anyone to the hospital. He'd immediately checked in with his lieutenant, dropped his bunker suit with Jax then grabbed a ride to the hospital from a PD officer.

"Lexi's friend, Melinda, saw her about two hours ago," Trent said as Logan moved to the side to answer his cell phone. "When Lexi told Melinda her suspicions about Patton, she suggested Lexi talk to a doctor named Lambert. He's the attending physician in charge of the residents, so Melinda thought he might be able to help."

Okay, that was new. "So, had Lambert seen her?"

Trent shrugged. "I don't know because he's missing, too. According to Detective Maxwell, neither one of them was caught on the security cameras anywhere in the hospital."

Shit. "What about Patton?"

"He's in custody," Logan said, coming back over to join them. "He's claiming he had nothing to do with the three deaths we're investigating, or Lexi's disappearance. Unfortunately, he's also starting to go through withdrawal symptoms from whatever drugs he's been taking, so I don't know if we can trust anything he says."

"Did anyone see Patton leave at any point before Lexi and Lambert went missing?" Dane asked.

Logan shook his head, but before he could say any more, his cell rang again. "I gotta get this."

"They're going to find her," Trent said as the detective answered his phone. "Detective Maxwell told me they're scouring the entire hospital for any sign of her or Lambert and they have BOLOs out, too. She's going to be okay."

Dane nodded, his chest tightening more with every passing second. He had no idea where Lexi was, but his gut told him she was in trouble. And all he could do about it was stand here and pray Logan and the rest of the cops found someone who might have seen something useful. Dammit, he hated standing around like this!

"We've got something," Logan announced.

Putting his phone away, he ran down the hallway. Dane followed, Trent right on his heels.

"What is it?" Dane demanded. "Did you find her?"

Logan shoved open the metal door to the stairwell and headed down the steps. "No. But we found the man who appears to have been the last person to handle those three missing bodies."

Dane wasn't sure what any of that meant for Lexi, but right then, he was willing to take what he could get.

When they reached the basement level, they found two uniformed officers standing beside a nervous-looking hospital employee in a white uniform. The guy was slim with a mustache and beard and curly dark hair.

"This is Jacob Taper," one of the officers said as they approached. "He's an orderly who works in the hospital morgue. He's responsible for bringing down the bodies from the upper floors and managing them until the attending physician signs off on the necessary paperwork. He also handles most of the transfer paperwork and occasionally transports the bodies to funeral homes or the ME's office if they can't pick the bodies up themselves."

The other officer slanted Taper a hard look. "He also seemed damn eager to leave when he realized what we wanted to talk to him about."

"I wasn't eager to leave," the man protested. "I was heading to dinner, that's all."

Logan ignored the man. "Did you read him his rights?"

When the two officers nodded, Logan turned to regard Taper.

"You're completely within your rights to stand there and say absolutely nothing, Mr. Taper. You may call a lawyer as soon as we're done booking you."

The man's eyes widened. "You're arresting me? For what? I haven't done anything!"

Logan continued as if he hadn't interrupted. "But if you remain silent, or you invoke the right to counsel, then we'll have no choice but to charge you as an accessory to the doctor's crimes. Forget all the stuff related to the desecration of a corpse, abuse and illegal transport of a corpse, and black market organ harvesting. That's chump change compared to the three counts of accessory to murder you're looking at. Those charges by themselves will put you in prison for life. And if we find out you were involved in the disappearance of a paramedic and a doctor, you might be looking at the death penalty."

Taper had gone pale before Logan was halfway through the list of charges. By the time the detective brought up accessory to murder, the orderly was hyperventilating.

When Logan mentioned the death penalty, Dane thought the man was going to keel over.

"Whoa, wait a minute! I didn't do any of those things," Taper said, holding up his hands like he was trying to keep Logan and the rest of them at bay. "The doc said the bodies were being donated to medical schools for education and research. He said that since those three people didn't have any family or insurance that their bodies would get cremated and interred in a potter's field somewhere. It seemed like such a waste, so when he asked me to help him, I agreed. He slipped me a few bucks, but all I did was fudge the paperwork then look the other way while he took the bodies." He swallowed hard, his Adam's apple bobbing up and down. "I swear I don't know anything about a missing doctor or paramedic. I came into work a couple hours ago. No one tells me shit down here in the basement. I don't even know who's missing."

Dane felt his heart sink into the pit of his stomach. He was half a second from slamming this jackass up against the wall and threatening to send him to the morgue he worked in. "You're saying Patton trusted you enough to help him get rid of three bodies, but when it came time to get rid of two more people, he asked someone else? I'm not buying that shit."

Taper looked at him in confusion. "Um... What are you talking about, dude? Patton's a dick weed and wouldn't be caught dead down here. He's not the guy who wanted those bodies for research."

Logan frowned. "If Patton isn't the doctor who paid you, who is?"

Taper looked even more confused. "Dr. Lambert."

Logan had his phone out before he reached the stairs. "This is Maxwell. I need everything you have on a doctor here at county named Arthur Lambert, and I need it yesterday. Then I want a BOLO put out on him, but advise caution. The man may have a hostage with him, a DF&R paramedic named Lexi Fletcher. I'm heading to Lambert's house as soon as you get me the address."

"I'm going with you," Dane announced, following him.

"Me, too," Trent added.

Logan didn't even look at them as he ran up the stairs. "Fine. Don't get in the way when we reach Lambert's place. If things go to shit, I can't be worrying about you two and Lexi at the same time."

Dane nodded even though he had no plan to do anything Logan suggested. If Lexi was in danger when they found her, he was going to get her out of it. No matter what he had to do.

Chapter Thirteen

LEXI WOKE UP with a godawful headache and a sore neck. She squinted against the light, closing her eyes for a moment as she tried to figure out where she was. She remembered Lambert jabbing her in the arm with a needle then lowering her to the floor...then nothing.

She opened her eyes again, more slowly this time. She tried to lift her hand to push her hair back from her face, but it wouldn't move. Frowning, she shook her head to clear the last remnants of unconsciousness from her head and realized she was tied to a chair, her wrists bound behind her back. Panic surged through her as she discovered her ankles were secured to the legs of the chair as well.

Heart thudding, she struggled against her bonds. Lambert was the killer, not Patton. He was the one who'd taken the other bodies to do heaven only knew what to them, and now he had her. She had to get free.

But no matter how hard she yanked, all she accomplished was abrading her wrists. Whatever was holding her to the chair was too strong for her to break, and too tight for her to slip out of. Her fingers and hands were already numb—so were her feet, for that matter. How long had she been down here?

Lexi took a deep breath, forcing herself to calm down. She was a paramedic, for heaven's sake. Freaking out wasn't going to help anything. She needed to figure out where she was and what kind of immediate danger she was in.

With that in mind, she lifted her head and let out a startled yelp, almost tipping the chair over as she tried to get as far away as possible from the disgusting scene set out before her.

In front of her was a meticulously set dinner table, complete with a white linen tablecloth, fancy silverware, and a holiday dinner. There was even a big turkey sitting in the center of the table. It looked so perfect, she almost thought it was fake, but the smell couldn't have come from anything but a real bird. Along with the turkey, there were the traditional holiday fixings—cranberry sauce, gravy, vegetables, and biscuits. There was no way she'd been unconscious long enough for someone to cook all of this...right?

But it wasn't the food on the table that really attracted her attention. That privilege was reserved for the three dead people sitting around it with her.

Wayne Moore sat to her left at the head of the table, dressed in a retro mint-green leisure suit. Debra Wallace sat to her right at the other end of the table. She was wearing a red velour dress, her hands closed in prayer on the table in front of her. Jessie Strickland sat across from Lexi. He wore a T-shirt with Rocky and Bullwinkle on it, his lifeless eyes fixed on the turkey. Beside Jessie, another place was set at the table, but there was no one seated in the chair.

Lexi looked away from the eerie tableau and down at her plate. That was when she realized she wasn't wearing her DF&R uniform anymore, but a white ruffled peasant top and flower print skirt. Knowing Lambert had undressed her while she'd been unconscious was almost as disturbing as waking up to find herself sitting at a table with three dead people. Had Lambert done anything else to her while she was out besides dress her? And how long would it be before she ended up like Wayne, Debra, and Jessie.

It took everything in her to not lose it completely and start screaming her head off for help. Lexi had never considered herself a person prone to panic. In fact, because of her occupation, she'd always prided herself on maintaining a level head. But that was before she'd been drugged, kidnapped, stripped, and redressed, tied to a chair in a semi-dark room, and posed like a doll in an episode of

The Twilight Zone. The only thing stopping her from screaming was the knowledge that if she made a sound, Lambert would probably come back. She really didn't want that.

She forced her attention away from her dead companions and looked around the room. While the single chandelier positioned perfectly over the turkey on the table illuminated the tableau, it left much of the remaining space around her in shadow. The lack of windows and the heavy wooden stairs disappearing upward into the pitch darkness were a dead giveaway that she was in a basement, even though basements were as rare as hen's teeth in this part of Texas.

Lexi could make out two couches, a recliner, and a huge console TV to one side of the room, and beyond that, there was a small fish tank with water gurgling in it. She wasn't able to make out any details, but the whole thing looked like it came out of the 1970s.

She turned back to the silverware on the table in front of her, wondering if she might be able to somehow use it to get loose, when she heard the thump of footsteps on the stairs. She jerked her head up to see Lambert coming down the steps. He was carrying a big bowl of mashed potatoes, and he smiled when he saw her.

"Ah, you're awake," he said as he set the bowl down, positioning it just so on the table. "That's good. I was so worried the food would get cold while we waited for you."

The man's voice was so completely

casual and conversational that it made goose bumps rise on Lexi's arms. The urge to scream for help crept up again, but she pushed it down. Whatever she did, she couldn't provoke him. Maybe then he might not do anything drastic.

"You killed these poor people," she said softly.

He straightened, drawing himself up. "It was necessary. Besides, no one will miss them anyway."

Lexi's blood went cold. "Are you going to kill me?"

Lambert smiled warmly at her again, like he had that day when he was comforting her over Wayne's death.

"Of course not, dear," he said. "I'm going to save you from the fire."

She swallowed hard. "What fire?"

"The fire I have to start," he said in that casual, almost serene voice as he moved about the table, carefully adjusting Wayne's tie, gently patting Debra's hair into place, positioning Jessie's knife and fork just so. When he was done, he looked over the three dead people at the table then at Lexi. "Everything has to be perfect, like it was before. But, this time, I'll save all of you."

That's when it hit her. "Oh God. Your family died in a fire, didn't they?"

Lambert didn't say anything. Instead, he spooned out food carefully onto the plates, positioning the potatoes, green beans, and dressing as if getting them ready for a photo shoot. Then he picked up a knife and slowly carved the turkey.

"I was young, little more than twelve," he said in a voice so soft Lexi could barely hear him. "It was Christmas, and I was over at a friend's house, playing with the new toys we'd both gotten."

Lambert paused for a moment, staring off into the darkness of the basement, his eyes far away. "It's funny. I can remember in clear, vivid detail what every member of my family was wearing that day, but I can't remember my friend's name. Strange, isn't it?"

He turned back to the turkey, carving as if he didn't expect her to answer. In reality, Lexi wasn't quite sure he was even talking to her.

"It was getting dark when I finally ran home to have dinner, but I was still able to see the smoke billowing up from the back of the house as I approached. I thought it was coming from the fireplace, so I didn't pay attention to it. Not until I reached the front yard and saw the flames through the windows." Lambert placed perfectly cut slices of turkey on the plates. "I ran through the front door, shouting for them, but the heat was so intense that I had to stumble back outside. I ran around the back and went in that way. That time, I made it to the living room. I saw them sitting at the table. They weren't moving."

Lambert's eyes were almost glazed over

as he relived that horrible moment from his past. It was impossible to hear him talking about seeing his family die in a fire and not think about Dane. Their stories were so similar, yet Dane had become a firefighter, risking his life to save others from the same fate that had befallen his parents, while Lambert had become psychotic.

She wanted to ask why he was doing this now, after all these years, but realized she already knew the answer to the question. All it took was the memory of the media interviewing Lambert outside the ER triage area and asking him to tell them all about the amazing kid who'd saved his entire family from a house fire. That would have certainly been enough to set a person like Lambert off.

"I wasn't in time to save them." Lambert drew himself up, his eyes taking on a resolute, determined expression. "But, this time, I will save them. Then everything will go back to being the way it was."

Giving her a smile and a nod, Lambert turned and headed for the stairs. Crap, he was really going to do this.

"Stop!" Lexi shouted. "You can't do this. It won't bring back your family."

Lambert glanced at her over his shoulder. "Don't worry, sis. I'll be home from playing in plenty of time for dinner."

Lexi shouted for Lambert to come back. But he wasn't coming back. He was too far gone for that. She didn't know where in the house he was going to start the fire, but she had no doubt he was getting ready to do it right then.

Pulse pounding, she struggled against the bindings tied around her wrists, ignoring the damage she knew she was doing to her skin, but they still wouldn't give. Desperate, she jerked side to side and front to back, hoping the chair would weaken and break. If it did, she might be able to scramble out of her bonds.

She heard a thud upstairs, followed immediately by a sloshing sound that was impossible to ignore. Then the smell hit her.

Gasoline.

Lambert was dousing the first floor with gas.

Screw it. Lexi opened her mouth and screamed for help at the top of her lungs, praying there was someone nearby to hear her. If not, then she was going to die.

* * * * *

Dane heard Lexi's screams at the same time he saw flames flickering through the windows of the traditional ranch style home west of Garland. Shouting for Trent to get DF&R out there and that one of their own was in the building, he ran toward the front door of the house.

"Slow down, Dane!" Logan shouted, falling into step beside him. "We have a murdering psycho in there who's already killed three people. He won't hesitate to kill more."

Dane didn't care. The drive out here in Logan's unmarked police car through Friday night traffic had been torture enough. Now that they were here, there was no way in hell he was going to leave Lexi in a burning house, no matter what he had to do.

Dane kicked in the front door, slowing only long enough to let Logan enter the house first with his weapon drawn. He immediately followed the cop inside, trying to see everywhere in the smoke-filled room at once. Heat and the scent of gasoline rolled toward him in waves from a long hallway that he assumed led toward the bedrooms. All it took was one flash of flames to remind him that he wasn't wearing his turnout gear—or a SCBA.

"Lexi!" he shouted over the roar of the fire. "Where are you?"

There was nothing but silence in the roar of the fire, but then a shout came from somewhere down below them.

"In the basement!"

Her voice was hard to hear over the flames, but he knew without a doubt it was Lexi. Relief rushed through him.

"Be careful!" she added. "He's up there somewhere!"

Leaving Logan to worry about Lambert, Dane took off for the kitchen, praying that was where he'd find the entrance to the basement. If it was in the other direction, they were screwed. The flames were already too high to ever get through that way.

Dane found the door to the basement near the old-style refrigerator in the equally antiquated kitchen. Logan grabbed his arm as he yanked open the door. The detective was already sweating and gasping for breath in the heat and smoke filling up this side of the house. Thanks to the gas Lambert had used to start the fire, the flames were spreading way faster than they should have, even in a place as old as this one.

"I'll stay up here and make sure Lambert doesn't try to trap all of us down there," Logan said. "This could be a trap, so be careful."

"You, too."

Giving him a nod, Dane turned and raced down the dark steps. Within a few feet, the air started to clear and turn cooler, and he breathed it in gratefully.

The scene in the basement was like something out of a frigging horror movie. A single chandelier shone light on a table piled high with food. Three dead bodies sat positioned around the table dressed in retro-style clothing and staring unseeingly at the plates in front of them. Lexi wasn't in sight though.

Dane's heart pounded even harder.

"Lexi, where are you?" he shouted.

"Over here," she called from the far side of the table. "On the floor."

He raced around the table, forcing himself to ignore the bodies there. Lexi was lying on the floor on her side, bound to a heavy, wooden chair, the ropes around her wrists so tight her fingertips were starting to turn purple.

Jerking the chair upright, Dane pulled his Gerber rescue knife off his belt and cut the ropes around her wrists, upper arms, waist, and ankles. He worked as fast as he could, knowing the situation upstairs was getting worse by the second.

Lexi tried to stand the moment he cut the last rope, but immediately stumbled. Dane caught her in time, easing her down to the floor in alarm.

"My feet are completely numb," she said, panic in her voice. "I can't walk!"

"It's because you were tied up for so long. You'll be okay, but I have to get you out of here."

Putting his knife away, Dane scooped her into his arms and ran for the steps. As he expected, the fire was much worse upstairs, and he immediately began coughing and gasping for breath. In his arms, Lexi did the same.

He looked around, wondering where the hell Logan was. They had to leave—now.

Suddenly, a tall form emerged out of the smoke from the dining room. Dane was about to let out a sigh of relief, but then he realized it wasn't Logan.

"She can't leave!" Lambert shouted, running at them like an enraged linebacker. "Not yet!"

With Lexi in his arms, all Dane could do was drop his shoulder and brace for impact. But at the last second, two other figures darted in from the direction of the living room and slammed into Lambert, knocking the doctor across the room. Logan, Trent, and Lambert ended up in a heap on the floor. For a guy who didn't look like he worked out a lot, Lambert was damn spry Jumping to his feet, he ran down the stairs to the basement.

"The dead bodies he stole are down there," Lexi said in between coughs. "He killed all three of them and now he thinks he can save them. He's insane."

Dane figured that last part went without saying, and was more than ready to let the deranged killer try to save as many corpses as he wanted—not that Dane thought that was very likely.

Logan headed for the stairs. "I'll get him!"

"You don't have time!" Dane shouted. "This whole house is going up any second. There won't be enough oxygen left up here by the time you come back with him."

The detective met his gaze. "I gotta try. It's my job. You two go. Get Lexi out of here."

Logan turned and charged down the steps before Dane could say anything else. Dane would have gone after him, but Lexi was coughing again. He had to get her out of her.

He turned and nodded at Trent. "Lead

the way!"

Trent led the way out of the kitchen. Dane followed, cradling Lexi closer to his chest to protect her from the flames as much as he could.

"Hold your breath!" he told her then darted across the smoke-filled living room. The flames had engulfed almost the entire back of the house, and were racing across the ceiling even as he and Trent ran. The heat was so intense his skin tingled in pain before he'd made it a dozen steps. But he kept going, knowing that if he went down, Lexi would never survive.

When they finally reached the front door and burst into the cool night air, Lexi breathed it in as fast as he did.

Firefighters and paramedics were there to grab Lexi out of his arms the moment he stepped outside. Dane looked up to see six DF&R vehicles from stations 29, 57, and 58 all lined up along the street. Two dozen firefighters, including Jax, Kate, Kohl, and Tory, were already working to contain the fire.

"There's a DPD detective in the basement," he shouted. "He's in there with the killer."

Kate and Tory charged through the front door without hesitation, as two firefighters from the five-seven urged him and Trent toward the nearest rescue truck. When they got there, the paramedics from Station 29 already had Lexi sitting on a gurney. They were giving her oxygen and checking the abrasions around her ankles and wrists. Dane brushed aside the oxygen mask one of the men held out to him and instead ran to her side.

"Are you okay?" he asked urgently, looking at her feet for the first time and realizing she wasn't wearing shoes. The fear of what that sicko doctor might have done to her warred with the fear that she'd been tied up so long she might have sustained serious damage.

She pulled off her mask to give him a small smile. "The feeling in my hands and feet is coming back now. They're tingling like crazy, which is a good sign. I'll be fine."

He wrapped his arms around her, hugging her close. "Lambert didn't...hurt you...did he?"

She shook her head against his chest. "No. He drugged me at the hospital, and I woke up here, surrounded by dead people. I'm a little creeped out to think about him changing my clothes, but as bizarre as it sounds, I think he thought of me as his sister. He would have never hurt me."

"He would have burned you alive," Trent murmured through his oxygen mask.

Lexi nodded. "Yeah, there is that."

Dane pressed a kiss to the top of her head. "I'm glad you're okay."

He would have said more, but right then Kate and Tory came out of the house, Logan supported between them, an arm draped over each of their shoulders. There was no sign of Lambert.

Kate and Tory helped Logan all the way over to the rescue truck where Dane, Lexi, and Trent were. The paramedics from Rescue 57 immediately began getting oxygen into the detective. Kate pulled off her gloves, helmet, and fire hood so she could help the paramedics. Her face was etched with concern as she tried to calm Logan's coughs.

The cop looked over and caught Dane's eye, giving him a slow shake of his head. Dane took that to mean the detective hadn't been able to reach the doctor in time to save him. Maybe Dane should have felt bad about that, but he had a hard time doing it. Lambert had killed three people, and tried to kill a fourth.

"How did you two find me?" Lexi asked, drawing his attention back to the woman he loved.

It took a second for that reminder to sink in, but when it finally did, Dane found himself grinning like an idiot. It might be a little early on in the relationship to say the words out loud yet, so he figured he'd better keep them to himself. But it still felt damn nice knowing Lexi was the woman he was going to be with for the rest of his life—assuming she wanted him around.

"It's a long story," he said. "I'll tell you all about it later. Preferably tomorrow, when we're relaxing and doing absolutely nothing."

"Not gonna happen," a voice said beside

them.

Dane looked up to see Jax standing there, his SCBA mask hanging off and a big smile on his face.

"Why's that?" Dane asked.

"Because Skye and I are getting married tomorrow, and not only are you the best man, you also have to walk Skye down the aisle." Jax jabbed a finger at him. "And don't think that almost getting killed by some madman is going to get you out of either of those things."

Dane chuckled. "Wouldn't think of it."

Jax only stayed around long enough to make sure they were all okay then he and Tory went back to fighting the fire.

That left him, Lexi, Trent, Kate, and Logan alone with the paramedics. Dane sat down beside Lexi and wrapped his arm around her, holding her close. She rested her head on his shoulder, one arm securely wrapped around his waist.

"You scared me there, you know," he said softly. "I know we talked about your having every right to risk your life as much as I do, but I never intended that to include going up against serial killers."

"That wasn't really my plan, either," she murmured.

"Good." He tipped her chin up and kissed her gently on the lips. "Then let's agree to never do that again."

She smiled. "Okay."

After that, they sat there quietly,

watching their fellow firefighters battle the raging fire and appreciating the fact they were both alive, and together. Finally, the words he thought he should probably sit on for a while bubbled up to the surface, and he had no choice but to say them.

"Is it too soon to say I love you?" he asked softly.

"No," she said.

"Okay then. But to make it official—I love you."

"I love you, too," she said against his chest.

Dane caught Trent grinning at him through his oxygen mask. Mouth twitching, Dane ignored the paramedic and went back to holding the woman he loved as he gazed at the fire that was going to keep burning for a very long time.

Chapter Fourteen

LADIES AND GENTLEMEN, Mr. and Mrs. Malloy invite all of their friends and family to join them on the dance floor," the DJ announced after Jax and Skye had finished their first dance as husband and wife.

"That means everyone needs to get their booties on the dance floor and start shaking them!" Skye announced with a laugh as the music began to play again.

Around Lexi and Dane, guests got up from the tables that had been neatly arranged around the backyard of their ranch. Dane grabbed her hand and tugged her to her feet.

"Come on," he said. "Let's celebrate."

Lexi was all for that. After yesterday, she was more than ready to have a little fun.

Dane pulled her in and slowly moved her around the dance floor—probably a little slower than necessary. But she understood that he was still worried about her. They'd both spent half the night in the ER—with Melinda tending to them personally—and were still technically in the recovery stage. Her throat was still raw from sucking down all the nasty smoke from the fire, and her wrists and ankles were probably going to be sore for at least another week. In all honesty, she was fine, but Dane had risked his life to save her, running into a burning building knowing there was a madman inside and carrying her out through the flames. The way she looked at it, if he wanted to coddle her a bit, he'd earned the right.

As of this morning, Lambert's body still hadn't been recovered, but the story of what he'd tried to do was all over the news and the Internet. While everyone was saying the standard lines about Dr. Lambert seeming so nice and normal, at the same time, grim-faced reporters were busy recounting the horrible story of Lambert's childhood and his family's deaths, with special guest psychologists giving their opinions on what had made the man snap. Lexi refused to listen to any of it. She and Dane had lived through the ordeal. That was all she cared about.

Lexi smiled as she took in the other couples moving across the floor around her and Dane. There were a ton of firefighters and paramedics in attendance, not only from Station 58, but from several other stations as well. The way every station on the northeast side of Dallas had come together last night to help had been amazing. DF&R really was one big family.

"Do you need to take a break?" Dane asked as the song came to an end.

The worried look on his face was so precious, it nearly brought tears to her eyes. It was crazy to think she was so in love with a man she'd just started dating. But when it was right, it was right.

She shook her head. "I'm fine."

He nodded. "Okay. But the moment you start feeling tired, I'm taking you straight back to my place and putting you in bed."

She wrapped both arms around his neck and gave him a wicked smile. "I won't complain about that, though I doubt either of us will get any rest if you do."

His mouth twitched. "You are so bad."

"Maybe," she agreed. "But you like me that way."

He grinned. "I won't argue with that."

Lexi laughed. She was damn lucky to have found a guy like Dane, and she promised herself that she wasn't going to forget it.

"So, do you prefer outdoor receptions like this one, or inside?" Dane asked out of the blue, his question pulling her attention firmly back to the present.

Her pulse skipped a beat at the question. "Why do you ask?"

He shrugged and tried to look nonchalant as he guided her around the floor. "No reason. Just curious."

She smiled. "Well, in that case, if it's winter, I prefer indoors, but if it's summer, outside definitely works for me. Although there should be a back-up plan in the event of rain."

Dane considered that then nodded. "I'll keep that in mind."

Lexi told herself not to get too excited. He was simply asking. But then a little voice in the back of her head reminded her that he'd said he loved her after only a week. She got the idea that once Dane had made up his mind about something, he didn't wait around too long before he took action.

Still, she shouldn't get ahead of herself. He still had to propose. But that didn't mean she couldn't start looking for a wedding dress.

ABOUT PAIGE

Paige Tyler is a *New York Times* and *USA Today* Bestselling Author of sexy, romantic suspense and paranormal romance. She and her very own military hero (also known as her husband) live on the beautiful Florida coast with their adorable fur baby (also known as their dog). Paige graduated with a degree in education, but decided to pursue her passion and write books about hunky alpha males and the kick-butt heroines who fall in love with them. She is represented by Bob Mecoy.

http://www.paigetylertheauthor.com

Made in the USA
San Bernardino, CA
24 April 2018